EVERY NIGHT I DREAM I'M A MONK,

EVERY NIGHT I DREAM I'M A MONSTER

NIGHT I'M A MONK — I DREAM EVERY

FREEHAND
BOOKS

EVERY NIGHT I DREAM I'M A MONSTER

DAMIAN TARNOPOLSKY

Freehand Books gratefully acknowledges the financial support for its publishing program provided by the Canada Council for the Arts and the Alberta Media Fund, and by the Government of Canada through the Canada Book Fund.

This book is available in print and Global Certified Accessible™ EPUB formats.

Freehand Books is located in Moh'kinsstis, Calgary, Alberta, within Treaty 7 territory and Métis Nation of Alberta Region 3, and on the traditional territories of the Siksika, the Kainai, and the Piikani, as well as the Iyarhe Nakoda and Tsuut'ina nations.

LIBRARY AND ARCHIVES CANADA CATALOGUING IN PUBLICATION

Title: Every night I dream I'm a monk, every night I dream I'm a monster / Damian Tarnopolsky.
Names: Tarnopolsky, Damian, author.
Identifiers:
Canadiana (print) 2024041053x
Canadiana (ebook) 20240410556
ISBN 9781990601804 (softcover)
ISBN 9781990601811 (EPUB)
ISBN 9781990601828 (PDF)
Subjects: LCGFT: Short stories.
Classification: LCC PS8639.A76 E94 2024 | DDC C813/.6—dc23

Edited by Naomi K. Lewis
Design by Natalie Olsen
Author photo by Diego Altamira Olvera
Printed and bound in Canada

FIRST PRINTING

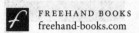 FREEHAND BOOKS
freehand-books.com

FOR MY FAMILY

CONTENTS

EVERY NIGHT I DREAM I'M A MONK,

EVERY NIGHT I DREAM I'M A MONSTER

TURTLES

I was playing on the computer past my bedtime, because they were fighting. Then it stopped, and there was no background to the beeping of the players on the pitch. I wanted to substitute the striker; he was injured. Then shoes on bare floorboards, and Mum pulling me up by the elbows, and me wanting to carry on playing because I was two-one up and it was the semi-final, and I'd never reached the final. She picked me up and carried me over to my closet — no, it doesn't make sense, I was too old for that. Too big. But that's how I remember it. She told me to get dressed and I looked at her. That's how I remember it, like the silence after a waiter knocks over a tower of plates, before the cruel cheers.

She reached into the huge white wardrobe. Half was my clothing and the rest was her overflow. She pushed back dresses and gowns and took out my best sweater and the navy pants I'd worn for my aunt's wedding and told me to change.

I looked over at my bedside table for my new Casio watch, I wanted to put that on first, I'd already taken it off for bed. She sat me down and roughly pulled the trousers on me, above my pyjama bottoms, and her neck and shoulders twitched. I took my Liverpool keyring from the table and put it in my pocket. I asked if Dad was coming.

I remember we took the Tube, but I don't remember the walk to the station. I can imagine trying not to step on snails in the dark. I don't remember her paying for the tickets. The blue and purple seats, the noise of the train shaking us back and forth, my terror of strangers as I looked for people my age, me trying to pull my sweater up so it would cover the space-ships on my pyjama top. Feeling for the keyring in my pocket. I hadn't worked out yet how to twist it onto my belt loops. Thin ads for travel agencies above the seats; the long low windows and the cables against the smokey brown walls; the multicol-oured noodles of the map. Yes, but first there must have been the wait for the train, she must have said something. I must have looked at all the white tiles, counting them. Which station did we go to? Probably I pressed against her. Maybe I cried.

Do you remember the Tube, Bella? We were kids. But what I don't understand about all this is where you were. Had Dad moved out and taken you? Were you at a friend's for the night? Why weren't you with me, Bella? Were you with Laura?

You can only betray what it's like to be that age. I don't know what it was like anymore. I've only got what I have here, in a whole other country. She wanted to change her life. She was younger then than I am now.

These dreams I have. These people I am.

At home I was never more than an inch from her side, but in public I hated holding her hand. What are we doing here? I kept asking. She pushed through the blue school doors — with rectangles of glass, and black lines on the glass so that they looked like graph paper. I bobbed behind her, in her wake. We were at the back of an auditorium. It was a third full, maybe, all old people. This bearded man was finishing a speech. I only remember his tone. The last thing he said was a question. There was something wrong with his voice. American? South African? We sat down in the last row just as they all started applauding and he thanked them. A lady who looked like the Queen of Belgium got up to thank him. Then they had two long questions that started with thanks. You couldn't hear the questions but you could hear love in them. It was far too bright in there for nighttime.

Mum looked about hawkishly, fidgeting with her purple cardigan, shifting her huge purse from one shoulder to the other, putting her hands in her hair. I only understood a few words, and you already know what they were: counselling for the heart of the family. Nurturing the secret self. The inner child and the art of life. The soul of the home. You know it, that whole seventies-eighties panoply. We have our own language for all this now. But the problems don't change. And I knew these people; she'd brought us all to therapists, to counsellors, to bring me out of my self, to make me speak, as if the problem between them was me, my silence, when all the time I knew and they knew that it was them, it was their words. I knew the warm eyes, the caring sighs. They'd given me crayons and animals and watched me play; they'd taken notes.

I leaned forward and scratched at the wooden seat-back nearest me, scuffed with ink, traced with my fingernail along the writing that was there, the names. Light blue cushions, the brown curtains at the side of the stage, the two awkward men up there, the white heads in the crowd nodding. Maybe I fell asleep for a minute. Then they were all getting up to leave. We'll wait for him outside, Mum said. She was looking at her lips in her little mirror, the one in the red and black leather case that snapped with a clasp when you snapped it shut. I said okay. Two-one, I was thinking. The final!

Then in the glass behind me all the suit jackets moving and parting, as I read off the names of the dead I'd never meet. She pulled me away and with the back of my head against her chest I was her icebreaking ship. A circle was gathering around the man who'd given the speech. They remained to congratulate him. She pushed me into the group, her hands grasping my shoulders hard. I tried to wriggle out. Seeing her distracted him, I could tell from how he looked over at us, but one of the old men talking wouldn't stop. He was saying the man with the beard had revolutionized him; he'd revolutionized his life. You've revivified me, he said, spitting as he spoke. He couldn't stop talking. He couldn't thank him enough. He held both his hands.

The speech man looked at me almost kindly. There was an ugly scar of red flattened skin on his lip and above, it stretched up into his curly brown-grey beard so no hair grew over the thin line there. A cow-faced woman clutching a magazine and a marker glared at me. I thought their shoulders were rounding into a wall as if to protect the speech man from us, like when you think the lights are going down and the ads and previews are going to start and you can have some popcorn, up to that point it's bad luck, so you don't. Mum let go of me and pushed ahead, and I was by myself among them, in a forest of waists and soap and leather purses.

I've brought someone, she said, interrupting.

He said something. I couldn't hear what.

She said, Appropriate? back to him and laughed like she was going to break.

Then her hand was gripping the inside of his forearm. He was wearing a tweed jacket. But under there, where your skin is soft, it would have hurt.

Helène, he said.

What you did is wrong, she replied sharply. You're a sick man, you know that?

He chuckled silently at his group, as if he'd just run into her and he couldn't believe the coincidence. He lowered his head and extended his hairy hand to lead us back and away, and with his eyes looking round the circle he asked gently to be excused. He seemed by his tone to be apologizing, sure that they understood, that there was nothing he could do. Behind him they made space.

Let's go in here, he said, and edged back easily.

He led us into a classroom. He sat on the teacher's desk near the front corner and one red corduroy leg dangled. I didn't look at him. I walked about under the posters of squid and antelopes as they whispered urgently and then hummed at one another. She embraced him, she was weeping into his shoulder. Then she broke away. He smiled at any action. I pretended that I couldn't hear.

There was a map of the world. I drew my finger along the blackboard, I picked up an eraser and blew on it. At my old school I used to get in trouble for eating pencil shavings, but I'd turned over a new leaf. This empty classroom, fluorescent lights, the speech I didn't understand, this school I didn't know — it seems like a dream now. But at the time I think I just took it all in, it was just another night of Mum. We could be swimming or burning clothes or I could be sitting in the car waiting for her for hours outside a community theatre or we could be here. I was already just as I am now. I don't change; I will never be *in thrall*. But I keep thinking that this is why we left England. I keep thinking, this is why she wanted to move back to Canada. It was just a few weeks later, in my head. Like I said the wrong thing, at some point, this evening. I know I must decipher this, but I don't know how.

Outside, through the small window panes with their white borders, the playground was black. I pictured a red-faced caretaker coming to throw us out.

No, there's nothing to doubt here. You might as well ask yourself if this moment is a dream, now. Dream of being understood. Dream of feeding the ducks in the park. But why bother? Dream that Bella, my sister, survived and didn't fracture her skull somewhere deep in the South Pacific and lives still. Dream that my daughter will speak to me again.

He had a careful voice, he paused a long time listening before saying anything. He must have noticed me looking at his disfigurement because he sort of smiled, half his lip moved up, and I didn't smile back.

From somewhere behind me she said, Mark, this is Dr. Anschauer.

You can call me Tony, he said.

Come over here and say hello, she told me.

Hi.

Come over here. Mind yourself.

I'm more like a friend, he called out. I'm helping your mummy and daddy talk about things. Sometimes friends forget how to talk about things.

Don't, she said.

He can know who I am, he replied mildly. He *should* know me. They all should.

You want to tell him the whole story then?

I grasped my keyring. Mum stood tight against one of the desks. I stayed where I was. I turned round and looked into the terrarium like everything was normal and fine. I'd started real school that year. We had uniforms and timetables and different teachers for different subjects, and on our walls were newspaper articles about real issues we were studying. I wanted to stay there.

I shouldn't have brought him, she said. God. This is all a mistake. What are we going to do, Tony? Tell me what you want.

It's all right, he said, watching me with a degree of interest that made me very aware of my clothes again, my pyjamas underneath.

She dropped her cheeks into her hands then immediately lifted her face up again. What am I doing here? she said slowly. She sounded tired again. Mark. I told you to come and be polite.

Why? I asked, in my head. But when I crossed those six feet to them she fell into a chair that was far too small for her and shook. Tony and I watched.

Do you like the turtles? he asked me.

They're tortoises, I said.

In fact I hadn't seen any.

Tortoises?

Yeah.

I guess I call everything turtles, he said.

My voice was too high; I wished it was lower, like my dad's.

We had some at my old school too, I told him, against my will. I'd never seen them at night. You lift them up and you move them around, and they stay where you leave them. They were soft inside.

I knew that next he was going to ask me what year I was in and if I liked my teacher. Orange spots speckled the walls and the ceiling like skin disease.

I always thought it would be nice to be a turtle, he said, singsong.

He lifted his eyebrows, as if he was waiting for me to say yeah or laugh.

After a while he asked me, What's in your pocket, Mark?

Nothing, I said.

Did you bring something with you?

Secretly I bit my lip hard.

I'd like to see, if you care to show me.

I didn't want to show him, really. But he got off the desk and went down on his knees and put his forearms on a table-top and rested his head on them almost sideways. His eyes beneath mine, his conkery scent, his TV voice, I don't know what it was. The flash of his white vest made him look like a priest. Unwillingly, I drew my hand out of my pocket and showed him the thin red wedge of leather with the medal, the golden bird.

My mum said suddenly, No, don't talk to him. We're going.

Liverpool fan, he said in a tone that I knew to be impressed.

I nodded. All my friends were too.

Arsenal man myself, he said.

I was sure that he was lying, that if I asked him their league position or to name their manager or top scorer or who they had next in the FA Cup he'd have no idea.

My dad's an Arsenal fan, I said.

Really?

He watched me carefully with great brown tea saucer eyes, like he knew I knew he knew nothing, but I didn't look away. I'd die before I looked away.

We're all looking for ourselves, he said. We're all on a journey.

My great secret was that I'd only become a Liverpool supporter that season. When I got to my new school, I'd switched allegiances because they were winning everything. I was worried that somehow he knew. So I told him who my favourite players were. I listed them off, to show that I was not fickle. Ronnie Whelan. Ian Rush. Men like my dad, or so I thought.

We have a plan, he said.

Don't, my mum interrupted.

The start of one. We think it's better.

Don't, she said more quietly.

He went on: I spoke to your father earlier. Now, your mother's a very special person. You know that. But grown-ups have to choose. It's part of the package. Would you like to live with us? Do you want to be part of the plan?

My mind was going a million miles per second. My fingers tightened around my keyring again. What about Bella? I said, but only in my head. He was watching me.

Are you old or young? he asked me at last. Or are you both at once?

Mum slapped the teacher's desk with both hands.

I get this image of our two faces, mine and this doctor's, both snapping sideways to look up at her. I can see myself. Me in my tight navy stovepipe pants, one hand in a tight fist at my side. What I looked like then.

I've looked him up. He's an old man now, with a storied past of a certain kind. His acolytes visit him in the nursing home; they genuflect before him. They say he saw the future, that we can live another way. Admittedly, there are gaps in his biography. Now there's a scandal: he founded a school, where he preyed on the boys. The teachers too. I wonder if she suspected something, even then. But I was tempted too.

He leaned closer to me then. He said, Mummy's feeling very—

Don't touch him! she screamed, and pulled me out of the room.

They were lovers, I suppose. I suppose she was trying to tell him something, by displaying me to him. She was younger then than I am now, whatever that means. How is such a thing possible?

22

Whatever it was between them didn't last. But if I ran into her on the subway, if I saw her on the street — at the age she was then, younger than I am now — would I think she was beautiful? Would we speak to each other?

She took my hand and, saying something to herself, she led me down the concrete steps. We walked back in the direction of the station and I stopped. Before, she'd promised we'd go home by cab. She said she didn't have the money, but I wouldn't move. You know what I was like, Bella. She looked back over her shoulder at the school. I thought she was going to start crying again, but I wasn't going to accept any change, any substitution. She'd promised. She sniffed water back up her nose, and my cheeks got hotter and hotter. To her, a child was something you moved around. You could put it anywhere. It could have been me, it could have been you. Whereas my own daughter, my Cassie, is concrete; her foundations reach deep into the earth. I called her when I got out of the hospital, one of my hospitals. I wish she'd call me back.

You said we were going to take a taxi, I told her. You said.

There aren't any. Do you see any?

It was starting to rain, and we were on a residential street, and the air smelled damp. Maybe two hundred yards away there was a pub, two ghostly black picnic tables, a main road. I looked but I didn't see any taxis.

It's late, Mark.

You said.

We walked, and every ten paces she walked out into the road and waited and looked and hailed cars desperately, and I shivered, cold and wet in secret. A thousand different cars went by and in the cavey orange street lights they all looked the same colour. When a taxi finally stopped I was satisfied for about a minute, then I started to feel bad. But I kept quiet.

I looked for cars with new license plates. I almost cried out when I saw a Lotus Esprit. She didn't say anything, I didn't ask her anything. She had a thumb in one eye and her fingers over her other eye and her nose, like a fan, like a bird's tail, like when she had a headache. She seemed to be far away. I was exhausted, my whole body.

I made myself small and held myself against her. She'd pulled her window down the height of a tea mug and her woollen cardigan was cold and rough against my face. When we turned, the force of it pushed me away, and then I'd crash back against her, but she didn't react. I looked at the moon and wondered how it was always following us in the window, I wanted to know why it didn't stay in one place in the sky.

Every twenty or thirty seconds the fare leaped. When Dad paid for taxis — once in a while, when we went to Leicester Square or Highbury — he always stood outside, by the driver's window, fingers spreading out his bills wide like a conjuror, his cuffs white as white, the driver's round bushy face waiting at his elbow. He could do everything. I was scared that when we got home he wouldn't be there. Or that when I woke up the next morning she would be gone, that I'd have another, different mother in her place. That you'd be older, that Laura would be younger.

We're going to try, she kept saying. We'll reset.

I could see her very clearly now.

When we were almost home she put her arm around me, as if she'd suddenly remembered I was there. We were on the High Street, going past the video store. I pulled away. It was too hard for me to love her. I didn't want to do it anymore.

IN THE PARLOUR

"What will it be like?" Frank said.

"Like this. Better," said Lise.

"We won't have to worry about being seen."

"We won't have to worry about anything."

"We'll be just as we want to be."

"Just as we want," she said, and reached down to smooth his yellow tie. He gripped her hand for a moment, his long fingers tight around hers.

"Do you know what you'll say?"

"No . . ." he said, kissing her chapped fingertips.

"Dusty," said Lise, pulling her arm away, back to herself. "We'll sit like this, but outside. There's the river, over there are the reeds. The sun drifts past our rowboat. We'll lie here in the middle of Central Park. I'll practise my lines and — What will you do? You can play all the other parts. Then we'll walk over to a bar we know. Fifth Avenue. I'll say: Landlord! Bourbon! With soda for my wife! And he'll nod. Just clearing my nerves: audition on Broadway. We'll walk there together.

I go through the back entrance to the studio. There's nothing like Broadway here. Do you see it?"

His chin trembled for a moment.

She smiled down at him.

"Treat it like a part," she said. "Play a role."

Frank pulled a slim silver cigarette case from his pocket, the one his father had dismissed as ladylike, and lit one cigarette. He touched the diamond-shaped emerald at the centre. He watched his smoke curl up, dodging the motes in the light of afternoon, then watched her watch him and smiled his hopeful smile, touching at a black strand of hair that eased past her temple and fell down along to her cheek. Their eyes met. There was no sound. Years later she would remember that, the silence.

"Are you packed?" he asked, his voice quieter.

"My bag is shut tight under the stairs."

"But Lise, could we just go now, and not say anything?"

"You said you owed it to him."

"But it will be such a scene. And his heart."

"It's up to you," Lise said firmly.

He turned and looked out of the scuffed window over the plane trees.

"We'll wait then," said Frank. "We'll do it like this. As we decided. And then straight to Union for our train." She came up close to him next to the window and held him. He told her, "You see, Lise, I'm not a dreamer."

"I've never known anyone like you," she said.

It was true.

"You make me see a different world."

30

He makes her laugh. He always has; he always took her seriously, before anyone else ever did. From when he was the master's son, and she was the girl in the scullery, three years older than him. She was always looking for someone; he was always running from his father. His father, who glared up at her when a sharp comment about Laurier slipped out as she piled up the tea silver that one evening, who arranged for his son's tutor to give her lessons in mathematics and French, and then as abruptly cut them off, because in this house his whims were law.

Lise let Frank go and pushed her hair back and picked up the *Evening Telegram* off the arm of the couch, smoothed it down, took it over to Frank's father's desk.

"Now then, what are you doing?" Frank said.

"Oh," she replied, grinning. "Oh of course." She retied her short apron.

"Come on, now. You'll never have to do that again," he said.

She bent a little so that he might kiss her comfortably, because she was taller than he was. He reached behind her back to untie her apron, and when they left off kissing, he made it a bundle in her hands, a bouquet.

"I can see up your nose," he said, and she batted him away.

Frank leaned back against his father's desk. When George Cohane comes home from work, he continues to work, after dinner, in here, in the parlour. In the parlour: the room where you go to talk. Frank, who was a noisy long-armed boy, started hiding himself in the kitchens to avoid the daily scene in which his father stood up from his desk to silence him with his belt.

They have sewn the wind, the reverend said on Sunday morning, they shall reap the whirlwind. Frank, a teenager then, looked at his hat between his thighs. He repeated the rich words silently. He was in love with the sound, the echo.

Now he swung his stilt-like legs back and forth, and he picked up a decorative stack of gold coins, all stuck together into one pile, that had always fascinated him. His father's Habsburg teacup with the scowling black and red birds. He ran the nail of his little finger around the honeycombed rim.

"No more being careful," he said. "I can't wait."

"Do you want to practise what you'll say?" Lise asked him. "Is there time?"

He stretched his arms out, and when she was a step closer, he caught her up.

"He'll be here at any moment. *After*," she finished daintily.

"After?"

"After, there will be no one but us," she promised.

"Just us. But you're right. Not in front of Mama."

Two identical faces watched them from over the couch, near the fireplace. It was as if his mother and father were twins, or as if the artist only knew how to paint the one face, unrelentingly determined, eternally disappointed. There was a baby in a frock sitting perfectly upright in a chair as no baby ever has, and an older boy in a stiff suit.

Frank had stood next to his mother on a rattling bridge in High Park, dropping twigs into a stream, and then rushing to the other side, terrified that they were gone forever.

"How did you become so wise?" he murmured into Lise's hair.

She didn't seem to hear, but then she said that she was not.

His older brother had died in the war. Frank had been too young to serve (though he knew boys in Grade 10 who joined up regardless). He was clattering around in the front hall looking for an umbrella to take to the Varsity game. He'd suddenly seen her, as if for the first time, and his face stopped. Her mother was the cook. He recognized the small green hardcover she was holding, a schoolbook he thought he'd lost, poems by Longfellow. At that moment, as he stepped towards her with palm open, there was a knock on the door, and a thin uniformed figure with a round tan hat, blurry through the glass, a boy his age calling out that he had a telegram.

The clock struck six.

"He'll be passing the corner now," Frank said, voice straining to be light.

"Don't be thoughtful," she said.

His eyes clouded. He looked suddenly bereft, like a toddler deprived of a rag he loved.

"He will rage," she said.

"I know."

He closed his eyes as he'd been taught to do before coming out on stage. Close your eyes, look inside to find your breath and find your voice. You can't just play the role; you must be the character. But as he reached eight in his head she took his hands in hers. Her round fingers and his long ones.

Somehow it gave him a sudden terror: his father kissing Lise. Talons cutting her to shreds. His heart pounded as a glob of hot urine squeezed out unbidden into his underpants. She laid out their clothes each evening.

"Oh God," he said.

"We'll withstand!" she said.

Do you ever feel that your life is small and fragile, a thing that you could drop, a blue glass jewel that could break into a thousand pieces at your feet?

He said: "I've disappointed you before. I won't disappoint you again."

"I love you," she told him.

This is the moment before, Frank told himself, putting out his cigarette in his father's ashtray. The players assemble. The audience settles. This is the wonderful, impossible moment, the moment of opportunity, he thinks, trying to believe it, when all is prepared, and nothing is known. At last he smiled his smile.

Lise kissed his hairline. He was trying to grow a moustache, to look older.

"I was born in the kitchen," she began. They heard footsteps in the hall, and Frank sprang from her. "You've already given me more than I ever imagined I could ever have," she finished, seriously.

"He's early!" Frank hissed.

When George was Frank's age he took barmaids to cheap hotels near the railway station. He left them bloody and in tears without a second thought. So he raised an eyebrow, seeing Frank spin away from his housemaid like a music box ballerina.

"Didn't think you had it in you," he almost said.

He went to his desk and his evening paper, with Frank at attention.

34

"That's a truly ridiculous tie, Frank," George said, without looking up.

Moustache brush, he thought. He couldn't find it this morning. Surely Frank hasn't taken it.

New elaboration of the Polish question. Plans for municipal rinks. No snow in forecast.

"The menu for the evening, Lise?"

She said, "Fricassee," and his jaw clenched.

George's fingers searched through the letters in the rack, while his other hand sought for his ivory letter knife. He pressed his belly against the desk. Two thousand miles of wire a week: the breadbasket must be fenced in again every ten years. This afternoon he clapped a hand on the minister's shoulder as he signed the contract: his fountain pen disappeared into his friend's pinkish fat hand.

"There's something I need, that is, something I would like to discuss, Father," Frank said.

"You can leave us," George told Lise.

He should be on his way to the club he knows on Parliament, where the girls are younger even than Lise. They giggle out a name, and each week it's a different name, and they are so tiny beneath you, and so firm. He even left the office early, a cigar pressed against his heart. But then he'd remembered that damnable fool Jervis was coming to see him about his fundraising committee for the new organ at St. Agatha's ... And now the boy.

George sighed. "Money for books, is it, Frank?"

"No, sir."

"You're not getting money for the theatre."

"No, sir."

George noticed Lise rearranging the glasses by the drinks cabinet.

"Still ailing with your *summer cold*, are you, Frank?"

"It's not that, Father."

"You need fresh air."

"Yes, Father."

"Well, what is it, boy?"

"I want, Father, that is, I wish to discuss my future."

George looked up, raised one steel eyebrow. His hands went to the pockets of his waistcoat. He looked again at Lise, but Frank spoke over him.

"No, Father, I want her here."

George was prepared. In fact he felt it was something he'd seen performed already: a tired Christmas pageant at the boy's school, the little plays his son used to put on in an elf's hat. Frank's pale cheeks, Frank blustering, confusing his lines and forgetting his motives, Frank spitting as he spoke, plainly clueless as to how he'd found himself on stage, as George looked around, a little bored, to see if there were any pliant mothers in need of accompaniment or control. George felt like a schoolteacher hearing a lesson for the twentieth year in a row as Frank went through his little routine. That he was a man now, not a boy (there's a laugh). That George had mapped out his son's life like a transaction (if only he had). The time he locked Frank up in his room for three days for some recalcitrant act (would he never forget that?). The inevitable presentation of the maid as fiancée. The final brandishing of the train tickets.

36

The exultant kiss. The two of them standing before him, bright and golden. Was he expected to toss a coin into his son's hat now?

George stood up, slowly, appraising them both in a single glance, and then he applauded. Slowly again, rhythmically.

"Quite a speech," George began, and took in the fear passing across his son's face, as when a dog steps backwards, awkwardly, into its space beneath the lowest shelf in the cupboard, to hide from the whip. His moustache rose slightly as he smiled.

"Quite a speech. Did you help him, Lise, learn his lines? You little whore."

He spat on the carpet.

Frank's cheek twitched, as it used to when he was little, at breakfast, every morning, when he had to tell his father he had wet the bed again, night after night, every morning for three years after his mother's death, and every morning the belt as his prize.

"You drab," George said. "You whore. You grew up in my house, and this is how you repay me? I pay for you to be educated, like a fool. Do you think anyone else would think it worthwhile, to spend good money on a spindly kitchen maid? And look at where it's got me." A dismissive gesture with the right hand. And then, growing louder: "You see a wallet. You see a way out. Smart girl. You learned just how to worm your little ass for him and make him hot, and he knows no better. You put your hands on your hips. He wants to wallow in your filth for a while?"

He spat again. His face was red, his finger trembling and pointing.

"Enough," he growled.

He came out from behind his desk slowly, he came very close, he loomed over them.

"You're not going to New York with my son. You're not going to be married. You get your bags, you pack your possessions, you take nothing from me, and you leave this house. Enough of you. Enough of your stench. Get out. And see how your life goes, girl, in this town, without my roof over your head, without me to protect you. Let's see what you become."

Close to her now, he breathed in. He raised his hand, and she stiffened. He traced the line of her cheek with his round, jewelled, fourth finger. He whispered to her.

"I had you marked out for myself, you know, but I let it pass. I was too good. I should have just had you when you were twelve, and none of this nonsense would have come about. You were tall already then, and dark, to my taste." Suddenly he was shouting: "Get on your knees, girl. On your knees! And beg my forgiveness."

Lise took Frank's hand.

*

Years later, in the middle of another war, forearms stained red in a tin tub full of cow's blood deep on a farm outside Bowmanville, a widow now, Lise will see this moment again. It's true that she grew up expecting nothing. She grew up a reader, and really she was a girl, and what would their lives have been like?

38

I still call him the master, she thinks. Though I have children of my own, grown boys of my own, and what unearthly danger are they in now? She wipes her forehead against the cheap fabric near her shoulder. A strand of greying hair drops against her white collarbone.

The blue sky seems infinite and there's a novel by Elizabeth Bowen waiting for her on an old unsteady table in the farmhouse, and she longs for the impossible, for her sons to be getting their fiddles out when she comes in so that they can play and sing. For the kettle to be whistling. For a cake to be cooling on the counter. To rest with them. For what cannot be.

*

He put his hand over his heart. He looked at them, bemused, then took two or three steps back, stopped like a drunk looking down for his boots, and then fell forwards onto the sofa, landed on it heavily, sideways, turned himself so that his face was down, the leather squealing, half his moustache pressed against it. He was breathing loud, as if his lungs were a mechanism, a faulty part.

"Father!" Frank said, letting Lise's hand drop as he jumped away. Her fingers stayed like that, parted.

"Help me move him!" Frank called to her.

He was kneeling on the floor, his yellow tie just licking his father's face. He took his jacket off, and Lise saw his bright red braces. The master was very pale, his eyes white and large.

Lise helped him turn the body. How hard he was! She smelled Frank's scent and the old man's sweat, and two colognes, one citrusy and one institutional. She felt the weight of the old man on his back like a whale ashore. But his face was clammy. Frank laid his jacket over his father's chest. The old man's empty cold eyes stared fixedly up at the portrait of himself with his family.

"What should we do?" Lise asked.

"Go and send for the doctor, Lise! Call him!"

Then the sick man spoke.

"I am all right," he whispered. "I am unharmed."

"Lise!" Frank repeated, panic growing in his voice.

"Just a rush of blood to the head," he mused in a tuneful, stuttering, and frightful way, a sound like a child playing the piano in the middle of the night, a voice they had never heard before. "I was dreaming," he said.

Frank pushed his head down against his father's side, forehead in the leather.

"Father! Father! Be well!" he cried out.

"Water," said the old man weakly, and Lise stepped fast to the cut glass. She listened to what Frank was saying now.

"Have you had more episodes, Father? Why don't you tell me? Dr. Lindbaum says you must tell me, Father. Why don't you trust me? Don't talk. You have to rest. We're going to call Dr. Lindbaum, and he'll see to this, Father, and it'll be nothing, you're just a little light-headed is all. Hush, Father. Drink this. Drink. You're not yourself. Have you been taking your tablets? Have you?"

George's collar was pushed up against his face from his fall. Frank eased it away from his father's lips to gently pour the cool water into his mouth.

They looked into each other's eyes.

"You're strong, Frank," said George. He paused and wheezed and waited and went on: "You're strong for me."

An hour passed.

"Frank," said Lise quietly, and then again.

"What's taking him?" he scutted.

"Did you hear what he said?" she asked Frank.

"Is Dr. Lindbaum coming?"

She said calmly, "Don't you see?"

"What, Lise —"

"Don't you see what he's doing?"

Frank with two hands on his father's chest, looking over his shoulder at her, as if they had just bumped into each other outside Eaton's and apologized, each of them carrying parcels, each of them on their way.

She had called five times. Now she put the telephone receiver down and came close to him, she pulled at his arm. She put her lips in his hair. She said, "Frank, remember. Remember *after*." She could hear the nervousness in her own voice. She rubbed her temple against his sleeve.

She said, quietly, "It's a trick, Frank. He's pretending."

"No, Lise," he said. "Please try to be quiet."

"We withstood, Frank," she said. "We withstood!"

"Please, he's resting now —"

She kissed him, an inch from his father, wrenching his face to hers, feeling him respond, feeling his blood begin to pound against her hands against his neck, the doubt in him quelled, feeling him rise towards her.

And then the doorbell rang. And Frank freed himself from her, knocking her back into sitting.

"Would you get the door, Lise!" he said, wiping his mouth on his sleeve.

"No, the train, Frank," she insisted. "The train is leaving. I'm going to the train."

"Someone has to get the door, Lise. I can't leave him like this."

"We withstood, Frank!" Lise said, but he said nothing.

She edged back away from the couch and away from the master's desk, into the centre of the room, unwillingly.

"He is *watching* me, Frank," she said, terrified now of a future whose shape she could not see.

HENRY'S
BAIZE SUIT

After their father's funeral, Daniel and Henry walked up through the village toward the house. They walked up the High Street, past the chemist's and the statue of Hardy looking at the Freemason's Arms, walking on a grey day that wanted to rain. Daniel nodded to people he knew and occasionally motioned to Henry, pointing out some new shop or set of traffic lights, a house dotted in the far fields visible through the spaces between buildings. Things that had sprung up in the five years since Henry had left home aged sixteen. It was March and still cold and Daniel breathed out and saw his breath vanish as he walked through it, saw his cigarette-faced brother's ungrieving smoke cling in the air. Father had smoked too; so they had had something in common, although Henry of course would never believe it. A single cigarette late at night, Daniel had found out towards the end, the time Father had looked up at him coming into the study unexpectedly and said, "My only sin," and laughed and coughed into his book. "I feel his hands around my neck," thought Daniel now, feeling older than his deflated twenty-six. "I miss him. How do you feel?"

They came to the house they'd grown up in, the chalk ice-berg at the top of the hill. In the kitchen Daniel filled the kettle and his brother grabbed a beer from the fridge. He raised the emerald bottle and looked up at it. "To our illustrious dead," he said and drank sourly. "To our illustrious dead dad," he intoned, and drank again and burped. He went up the stairs, and Daniel poured out half the water from the kettle to hurry it and started on the dishes left over from breakfast. He could hear his younger brother's steps through the ceiling. Already last night Henry had started weighing and dividing, picking through possessions upstairs. Mother's things, the things he'd never really known. Father's things, things Father hadn't shared with him. At least now he was wearing Daniel's second suit so he'd look decent doing it, at least he'd look like a refined burglar, whatever he actually was.

"Wonder if he'll give me back the trousers though, or just keep them. Three days," Daniel thought. "If I were his age I'd be no better though. He only looked angry at the grave-side. But he kept quiet. Father would have liked the crowd. He wouldn't have taken Henry's arm. Dead dad."

Forgetting his silent cup of tea Daniel looked out at the garden and listened to the tramping steps, thought about getting a fire on later. He wondered which room Henry was rifling through, but it was hard to tell from just the noises, with the water on too, hot and thick through rubber gloves. Then he heard Henry drumming the stairs hard on his way down before he appeared in the doorway. Henry smiled at him, elbow on the doorframe like a dandy. "Fancy a game of snooker?" Daniel looked back at him blank faced.

As Henry flicked on the lights, Daniel, coming after him, made his way into the basement room. It spread wide around him, nicely done up with a Victorian panelled elegance. It was the only room big enough to accommodate the table and had an uncomfortable style, its private-club feel mixing with the dank atmosphere underground. It felt like the inside of a plush coffin. Daniel pulled at the thick naval cloth that lay protectively and semi-permanently over the table Father had bought some twenty years before and watched the dust filter up to and past the long lamp above. Underneath, the great green sea of felt. While his brother rattled the scoreboard on the wall, Daniel breathed in over the cloth, still marked with the odd handprint from the last time he and Father had played, before the final illness. He thought what to say and said nothing. A quiet sea with its lines of latitude and rules of passage.

"New surface," noted Henry, marching over.

Of course it was.

"Smooth."

Daniel drew out the box of balls and opened it up and saw their glisten. Islands for each empty black spot marked on the table. Yellow-land, brown-land, and Henry had never laughed at this, green-land. He dotted them in the order learnt in childhood, down to God green Bless brown You yellow: with each in its place, the table glowed with a symmetry Daniel could bathe in. Playing so soon couldn't be appropriate, but still he felt the order was good. Three days, but the colours just sat there without words.

"I'm going to break," said Henry, cue in hand. He flicked the cue ball off the back cushion and stopped it at the line with his finger, next to the yellow. Daniel closed his eyes as he heard his brother crack the white against the triangle of reds. And then there was chaos.

It was five years since they'd last played, but they fell instantly into their old rhythm, Henry pursuing his insolent risks, pulling off mercurial shots and failing as spectacularly, abusing the rules and seeming to do it all with a case to prove. Daniel slower and usually ahead. Neither of them had their father's intuitive cold gift for the game. He'd never taught them to play his way, that was impossible, but they'd watched and played in his shadow when they were allowed. Daniel remembered their last game and put the thought away, concentrating on a difficult red to the corner, leaning towards the ball in a hunchback pose. Looking up at the pocket and down at the red, up at the red and down at the white, the cue moving an inch forward and an inch back in preparatory motion governed by his interior metronome. "Done this before," he thought. "This old angle." That should have made things easier, but it was no easier if every shot felt like an anniversary. As the cue moved forwards, he saw Henry leaving a new bottle of beer on the rail. If it fell. Daniel missed and Henry potted the ball, moved like a sharp jackal around the table, knelt to look at things from the pocket's perspective.

"I want the Brodi from the study," Henry said as he stood up.

Daniel's mouth replied. "You want it?"

"Yeah."

"But we —"

"Do you want it?"

"I don't know, Henry. I mean it's only been three days."

48

"It's been five years." Eyebrow cocked into the pause between them. "Twenty, depending on how you approach things. I might sell it."

Henry had talked vaguely about his businesses the night before. This after he'd arrived late, driven up by a man the size of a boulder, in a car that was lit purple neon underneath. His head was shaved now and he snarled even when he was sitting on the floor, doing nothing, humming. His driver had been wearing a tuxedo. The pounding bass had shaken Daniel's ribs from the inside.

Henry sank the pink with clean emphasis and strutted around chalking his cue blue, ignoring the white ball as it bit back with the spin to where he wanted it. It rested near the 'D,' with a possible but difficult long red stretching into the corner. "Tell you what," he said, leering. "If I sink this red, I keep it. If not, you can have it."

"The sculpture in the study?" Daniel asked vacuously. It couldn't be the way to pay Henry back, if Henry could be paid back. It was too soon to be doing this at all, he thought. But say no? You couldn't rebuke Job for crying out. Henry was owed so much. "Got to pay him back somehow," his head said as his lungs forced a laugh. "What the hell," he said. "All right." Henry took the shot. He stayed there, forehead on his arm as the ball came back from the sides of the pocket.

"I only wanted it to smash it anyway."

Henry walked off to the scoreboard and stood there, moving the marker along as Daniel softly compiled a break. Watching the alternating pattern of red, colour, red, colour, Henry told a story he hadn't told before, of the afternoon he'd gone into Father's study five minutes early, at five to six. Five minutes before the rules allowed, for some excited reason he could no longer remember. And for five minutes Father refusing even to notice that he was there, sitting instead like bearded Moses if Moses had ever sat glowering whitely at his desk, ignoring the repeated diminuendo of his son's call. And Henry said he had wanted to destroy something of value right there just to make the old man look, and when he gave up and walked out, he walked by the little maternal bust on the mantelpiece, and he was this close to reaching up to it and pulling it over. But he didn't; he's regretted it since.

"He was always withdrawn after Mother died," said Daniel at the end of his brother's speech. Henry blew the chalk off his cue as a stockbroker might.

"Not always. Not with you."

"Like he wasn't himself anymore," Daniel mused. "Henry, you can keep it if you want."

"I missed the stupid shot. Carry on."

*

The game progressed and Henry kept placing bets on the outcome of shots, more wildly as they went. First he took their father's writing desk on a difficult green, and Daniel kept the piano on the last red. "Still lots to play for," said Henry. "Do you want anything from the kitchen?" He snorted as he went up to get another beer and Daniel saw him go off in the dress shirt, the jacket perhaps on the back of a chair somewhere, probably on the floor somewhere. We must look like something from an etching, Daniel thought, *Gentlemen Brothers Play At Snooker in Delightful Clothes.*

Being down there alone momentarily felt like times past when he'd practised. These last five years, after Father had had the table resurfaced, Daniel would come down and set the balls up himself, playing and waiting in case Father should join him. It wasn't the same playing by yourself when the game wanted two, but it gave you the same problems: you could have the finest ideas in your head, and you'd play the shot but so often you'd top it, or you'd misjudge. Or there'd be something you couldn't account for, some flaw in the way you'd been taught to hold the cue years ago, some flaw in the way the world itself was shaped. It would never go as you'd imagined, something would interfere and eventually your very ideas would be undermined; you were so unsure of being able to work them out on the table that they'd decay and become uncertain in your head, like waking up one morning and not knowing who you were, like waking up one morning and not knowing your own name.

Henry was shouting something from upstairs, which he repeated in the doorway with his drink. "I think we should play for the library then," he said, still testing.

"I think I've had enough of this game," said Daniel.

"Four thousand books — is it? — on a blue," his brother ignored him. "Two thousand leatherbound books."

"It's not a good idea." Neither of them moved towards the table.

"Don't want to lose them, do you."

"It's not that, Henry. You've got as much right to them as I have."

"Oh I do? Oh thank you."

"I didn't mean —"

"No, I mean you're the one who's read them. But if you want them I think it's only fair for me to have a chance, since if not you just assume them. Because I will fucking toss them out tonight, one by one. Lots of memories of evening readings I wasn't party to. Nice little bonfire."

"You're being melodramatic." The ball waited.

"Didn't you ever feel guilty to always get off so freely?"

Always.

"Henry."

"There's lots I wouldn't stand for now, from you or him. A person changes."

"Will you be quiet if we play for it?"

"Lots I wouldn't take."

"All right then Henry." Daniel leaned over the white. It was a difficult shot, the cue ball being stuck so close to the pink that the only way to approach it was by aiming over, holding the cue almost perpendicular to the table. That angle again. "Be careful now," said his brother. Daniel aimed the white towards the blue, and as the blue ricocheted in turn towards the pocket Henry took a step in and picked it up, rolled it the other way in a smooth motion. "Oh bad luck" he sighed. "Only fair though." Daniel's breath gathered heatedly in his chest as Henry took aim himself and potted the blue. "You've got to be careful when you're cuing at that angle. I mean, if you slip ..."

"This is what you wanted to talk about?"

"Suppose I have some reading to catch up on."

"Henry."

"That? The suit? I might have expected a severe beating or something, but hell, weren't you surprised?"

That night.

"Old Testament punishment. You have that Old Testament frame of mind too though."

Henry had been half-wasted that night as well and hadn't wanted to go to bed after he'd come from the pub. It was Daniel, though, who'd misjudged on a shot at that same angle and sent the cue scraping sharply into the baize. The rip's unfathomable voice had spun up through the house, through the empty kitchen and up the stairs again through the closed study doors into Father's cocked ear. The colours disjointed and not knowing what to do. And all the blood drained from Daniel's face. Henry had laughed and stepped forward as his brother stepped away, half fainting, and when the angry clatter turned into Father coming off the stairs the massive old man had only seen Henry grinning over a rip in the table, drink in hand.

"The reason I stayed the three days after he finally let me out of my room was because I was waiting for you to say something. I don't know how I managed three days. Didn't you wonder what it felt like? I actually thought you might speak up and admit to what you'd done, say something, when you saw what he was doing to me —"

As Henry spoke Daniel had the surreal recollection of his brother's stare, his brother staring at him from across the breakfast table, not eating, to the neck in green.

"Scratching at green sweat behind my kneecaps. And you wouldn't admit it. Course to me it was proof that at least he felt something for me even if it was just hate. Because to think to punish me at such lengths ... I wonder actually if Mother had been around if he would have. But she was always too sick once I came along, right? He wouldn't let me take it off even to sleep. A flap buttoned into the back so I could shit. I couldn't shower. Eventually I had to rip myself out with the kitchen shears. If you remember."

The table stood by itself between them. Henry started to trail off.

"A suit made of baize. Going to the tailor to make me a suit out of the baize you broke, just to teach me the value of it. Do you think I even would have put it on if I hadn't been waiting for you to finally say something?"

"What could I have said?"

"Anything."

"You don't think I was scared of him too?"

"You were friends."

"I'm sorry, Henry."

"You wanted to stay his friend too."

"Henry."

"Isn't it your shot?"

Pink and black left.

"Let's stop this," Daniel said. "We're not kids."

His brother stood between him and the door.

"Yeah let's stop this," Henry repeated back sarcastically. "Thirteen points on the table."

"I don't want to." Pink skin, black hair. Green suit.

"Pink and black keeps the house."

"Henry, I'm not playing this." Daniel tried to speak as severely as his brother, feeling the anger rise up through his throat.

"Pink and black for it."

"You can't play for a house."

"You played for the fucking piano."

"For God's sake Henry." They had moved closer together now. No one else was in the house. There was no one for miles.

"Pink and black."

"Henry."

"You're still on his side."

"Stop it!"

The yell surprised Henry. Daniel pushed him away as he lifted the cue and speared it down across into the table. He held the cue at its base and pulled up as if he were pulling some great fish out from the felt, and pulled again and ripped, scoring a Y, an X, into the surface. The sound ripped around and tore and died and Daniel stood by a broken mess of felt folded over its mangled self-possibilities, the grey hard unforgiving slate beneath.

He looked up at Henry over the ripped remains of their father's game.

"Please," he said. "Can't we just both start again?"

Submitted to the Hart House Annual Literary Contest, April 1st, 1999
Word count: 2,855 words
Author: Mark Ferguson
Email: mferguson@hotmail.com
Bio: Mark Ferguson is studying politics and philosophy at the University of Toronto.

BED

I had decided to take to my bed and announced to no one at all that I would no longer be going to my office, I would no longer be visiting friends, I would no longer be making a *contribution* to what is laughably called civil society, that I was taking to my bed and that being of sound mind my decision was irrevocable and pointed. There was no purpose any longer to being in the world, to doing things in the world, to breakfast meetings or *catching up* or concerts or charity functions, that these things were in fact, I had finally seen — how the scales had fallen from my eyes — that these things were in fact deleterious in the extreme, damaging and hateful activities that poisoned the mind, soul, and flesh and merited, in fact, only the most absolute refusal. So in my bed I stayed. Predictably my wife panicked, my doctor panicked, the world panicked, everyone panicked. I stayed in my bed, resolute. I refused to explain myself, I refused to defend myself, I said nothing, I watched them come and go with no little degree of wide-eyed pleasure, I had become a child again and each of them the rod.

My wife in particular — the poor creature — had no idea what to do with herself. From the first morning she was *helpless*, crying at my bedside to try to soften me, bewailing what had become of me, crying into the sheets and pulling at the blankets. All of which was a kind of mental laziness, I thought, and a hatred in her, her hatred of me, which she could only express by a kind of primitive caterwauling. For the sake of the children, I told her, be quiet. That shut her up, it always did. She had been saying, But why, but why, before that she had been asking if I was ill, if there was something wrong, before that she had been saying it was time to go to work, before that she had said it's seven, it's seven-fifteen, it's seven-thirty, you have to go, it's time to go. Helène, I said to her, I am happy. It is warm here, and the world is cold. I have lain in bed eight hours and rested none. All night I was awake and tense with my hands clenched. All night I was staring at the ceiling. This was true. All night I had been awake, listening to the motorcycles go past my window, listening to her breathing so loudly and ineptly and then *speaking*, I have a wife who actually converses in her sleep, this woman who is incapable by day or night of silence, whose chatter is unceasing lest she stop and be forced to, for the first time, confront herself, confront what she is, unless she actually might think, reflect, and by some miracle stumble into seeing what she has become and was always waiting to be. A voice like this! Can you imagine? How did my life become interwoven, I was thinking as I lay there awake all last night, with a woman who wears leather miniskirts, at her age? Who owns more handbags than she has gone to concerts? Who refuses to eat vegetables — vegetables! — because they are dirtied by the soil? (Oh how these little facts used to charm me! and now they have become rapiers and poniards sewn into my clothes.) All night I was awake, I told her, listening to your infernal mouth-chatter, and now I wish to be left alone, I wish to sleep, I wish to stay in the little warmth I have created for myself, alone.

The weeks passed. She called a doctor. She consulted my children (my eldest daughter was mad and rich, my younger daughter was clever and rebellious, my son was, I don't know what my son was, perhaps it was he who called the doctor after all, precocious little brat), who called a witless psychiatrist, who pulled a chair up to my bed and cleared his throat and asked me if I knew that my wife was concerned. Know! Know I said, how could I not, how could I be in ignorance, she weeps all day, she sleeps on the couch, all evening speaks she to her pathologically cretinous friends about me, of course I know, of course I know — and what's more, I'm rather concerned about her. She weeps all day, she sleeps on the couch, she has endless telephone conversations at the end of which she is less consoled than at the start — Doctor, I said, the woman needs your help, the assistance of a professional, if she is to regain her mental health, her thriving state, if she is to become again what she once was, my tower of strength, my little hussy — I winked at him, I took in his small goatee, he was drinking chamomile tea from my Habsburg cup, she had given him my Habsburg cup! Her father's cup, the one that she had presented to me, on our wedding day! My essence, my being. The one that had, at one point, according to some admittedly somewhat hazy family lore, been part of a set that a Rhineland elector-archbishop swapped for a regiment of dragoons! — Doctor, you have to help her. This was true. I was concerned about her. I had taken to my bed, but I had had no peace, because of her, because of her caterwauling. She received a telephone call from my office at the factory. They had not seen me, they said to her, I had not come in, they said to her, we would like to have a word with him. By all means! Come one come all! I said. I said I would have nothing to do with it, if they wanted to speak to me let them come. I wasn't going anywhere. Do you *often* make house calls? I asked the doctor, with authentic and genuine interest. I mean in this day and age.

The weeks passed. Mr. Sauer came to see me. Joe Ferguson, he said, we haven't seen you in the office in weeks! He laughed, he had no idea what to say to me. We had never spoken outside the office, not even on a single occasion, because we hated each other, passionately, we'd just needed the chance to express it. You are going to be coming back, aren't you, shortly? He was lining his nest, anyone could see. But of course! I said, but of course, it would be such a pleasure to see everyone again, Gord and Esta and little Ferdy. Unless of course they'd like to drop by and see me! Ha! I laughed. Ha! He laughed. We both laughed. I stopped first and looked at him, mouth wide, eyes closed, like an ape. He stopped laughing. But seriously, he said. But seriously, I said. When are you coming back to work, he said. Never, I said. Never. Why are you doing this? he said. I told him everything, I told him nothing. I can't go on, I said, there is too much, there is too much, and I can no longer be a part of it, I can no longer carry on with it, I can no longer contribute to it. I just want to remain here in my bed.

I don't want to act, I don't want to be a part of things, I don't want to work, I don't want to be paid, I don't want to be here anymore, I don't want to feel anything, anymore. It is all up with me, as the Russians say. Is it all up with you? he asked. They say that too, the Russians, I told him. You're not yourself, he said. Then who the hell am I? I asked.

The weeks passed. My bed, my taking to my bed gave me no little degree of local renown. *And just at the time I thought I was escaping from life I found myself more and more a part of it.* It began, though it wasn't the beginning, with the psychiatrist, who had mentioned my case — professional ethics! — to a friend at dinner, no doubt one of those awful dinners where the friends, who envy and despise one another, say things like, But there are no great figurative painters left today, not since Edward Dacres died, and ask each other about their books, about their paintings, about their films, about their patients — their patients! — their cases, their successes, their children in superior universities studying finance and planning to make fortunes and plotting how best to present themselves in court after murdering their parents. The psychiatrist, my wife's psychiatrist, had mentioned my case to his priest in the confessional, and he in turn had mentioned it to his sister at dinner (the seal of the confessional!) when she returned from her most recent "war zone experience," and she in turn mentioned it to a laughably stupid fellow reporter who arrived at my house with a cameraman and a microphone and barged her way to my bedside. So I was nice. I was very nice. How long have you been lying in your bed, she said to me after adjusting her makeup, her blouse, her blouse, her tight red blouse.

How long have you been lying in your bed? I told her two months, give or take. It might have been more, who knows. And what have you been doing in that time. What do you mean, I said. What do you do, to keep yourself occupied? Occupied! I said, Occupied, she said. Occupied, I said, now I understand. I'll keep you occupied, I thought. Nothing at all, I told her, I do nothing at all. I lie in my bed and I look at the ceiling. Now get out. I was being nice, but it is never so easy. Are you having some kind of midlife crisis? she asked me. No, I said, my doctor has given me a clean bill of health. Is this a bed-in? What, I said. Are you an anti-capitalist? I don't know what you're talking about. Is it art? Good God, I said, I hope not.

The weeks passed. The children flitted by in the corridor like ghosts. I was written up in the local paper, inevitably, that rag of gossip and vituperation and charity hospital openings and the local sports team (which sport? I don't care which sport!) and classified two-line advertisements for rebirthing therapy, and my name was mentioned in various portals and platforms that I'm confidently told by my son exist electronically only in the minds of people watching at them, gap-mouthed, vole-eyed. My fame spread, the bed-man I was called, the man who lies in bed. I was asked who I would be voting for in the local elections, in the provincial elections, in the parliamentary elections, in the senatorial elections, in the presidential elections, in the monarchical elections. Sometimes the telephone would ring and my opinion would be requested and even printed in some magazine. As if I had become a man of weight. Laughable. But it tickled me, because if there is something I am, apart from impatient, stubborn, selfish, misogynistic, misanthropic, unfriendly, and ungracious, it is narcissistic. And so with a certain degree of pleasure I watched my own rise as I would perhaps that of a sportsman or film starlet, waiting for the inevitable fall. In the meantime I toyed with the comforter, I pulled at its million frayed vermillion threads.

The weeks passed. A doctoral student came. He asked me if I was familiar with the writings of the Lethargists, who counselled that the life spent lying down was the best of all. Nope. He asked me if I knew of the work of Proust, who wrote, he said, in bed. Nope. He told me he was preparing a study of the bed in Western life in the early modern period and wondered if he might interview me further. Nope. My wife, my poor wife, my poor poor wife. She was hopeless, she was helpless, she didn't understand, she thought it was her. It's me, it's me, she said endlessly, you don't love me, you don't want me anymore. Want you, I thought, what for? Though it's true, if there was anyone at the top of my list of people I did not want, it was her; after, of course, me. Was it true? She was destroyed, she was losing weight, she wasn't sleeping, she was desperately unhappy. She had been unhappy before, she just hadn't known it. I had been unhappy before and I'd known it. Now I was happy, and I knew it. But she was unhappy. I knew that too. Did she know I was happy? Good question. I don't know. She was becoming slyer. It's not fair, she said, what you're doing. It's not fair: what makes you special, do you think, have you thought about it? she said. What are you trying to do? she said, To yourself, doing this, doing nothing? Do you think it's easy, my life? Sleeping on the couch, going out to work alone, coming back alone, no one to speak to in the house, eating dinner alone, why do you hate me so much? I don't hate you, darling, I said at last. I don't understand, she said, I don't understand how you can be happy doing nothing, how you can lie there and do nothing, day after day. Don't you want to be something? Don't you want to do something? No, I said, no no no no no no no. What do you think it would be like, she said, if everyone was like you? If everyone decided one little morning, ach you know, I don't feel like it today, I'm not going in to work today. If the police decided they weren't going to go in to work, if the ambulance drivers ... *Helène*, I said to her, *I make brassieres*. It's the principle, she said. What would people think of me if I was like you — I'm a laughingstock already, because of you — how would things be if I decided to go to bed, not to get up, to leave my life well alone, if I didn't cook, if I didn't care, how would you feel then? Be my guest, I said. Be my guest.

The weeks passed. Getting up every morning isn't easy, you know, she said, over her shoulder in the corridor now. What, I said, and looked across at her, looked away from the ceiling. I was staring at the ceiling, following the rifts in the paint. Do you think it's easy, and you've figured it all out, you being so much cleverer than all the rest of us? We're both effervescently fecal representatives of human mediocrity, Helène, I told her, you and I — I just happen to be lying down. Do you think it's easy? Do you think it's easy for everyone else, that you're the only one who's thought about it? Don't you think I'd like to spend a year in bed, just for the hell of it, just to camp out for a while? You wouldn't be very good at it, I thought, you're much too eager. Why do you think everyone is trying to make the world a terrible place for you, she said, from the doorway now. A mediocre banality, I said, a walking shithole. Can't you listen? Can't you listen to me? she said. It was four in the morning. Helène, I said, I can't do it anymore. I used to be able to do it, but now I can't. Can you think of a reason, of a single reason for me to get up? I don't want to be a part of it anymore, I want to break the habit, the only way to break a habit is viciously, all at once. Otherwise it lingers. What about money? she said. We have money, I said. My whole life I have been working for us to have money. We have more than we need. We don't need more money, you don't have to work, not for money. How can you just lie around and do nothing? she said, at the bottom of the bed now. How can you live without doing something? I am doing something, I said. And then I saw. That was the crux. Slowly I realized. There wasn't a way out, not in this life. Here I was, priding myself on refusing, on not contributing, and look at me shitting my way through the world, *making a spectacle of myself*. It would have been better to keep going. It would have been better to keep working. It would have been better to go on loving my wife. She would perhaps have been less viscerally unhappy. Perhaps; or temporarily. Though not in the long run. You can't get around that. Now she had taken to bed. Now she had joined me. And here I was. Showing off again as my wife lay next to me, speechless, over the covers. There was no escape for me, from me, from that, or from the others, those who had become part of me, those who had colonized me, my friends, the idiots, the saints, the imbeciles, their thoughts and feelings, handled and dirtied, passed on to me, and so they became mine, so briefly, so briefly, until I shat them out in my turn. Get up! I said, and she said, No. Get up! I said. I kicked the thin covers off my grey emaciated speckled spotted boney bonny shins, onto her. I stood, I tottered, I regained my footing, I limped to the door, I stood up straight, I looked back, over my shoulder, at her, lying there, so still. So still. I turned away. I heard the children coming home from school. I heard the key in the door.

And so the thing went on.

BIG FUZZY
SWEATER

I'm sitting in the living room mulling it over, with a glass of the red I just opened warming in my hand, trying to get lost in thought. When it's lunch you can handle things by drinking your way through it, I'm thinking, but dinner with a mushroom hangover is another story, you've been awake so many hours, you have to keep a low profile. Mom and Bella are in the kitchen. Dad's upstairs and Laura isn't here yet. I can hear pieces of what they're saying, Mom telling Bella to tie her hair back, she has such a pretty face. Take it easy on him, she says. The warm smell from the kitchen. Mom gets panicky when she's by herself for too long. That's what people say when you're big, says Bella. You have such a pretty face.

"How's school?" Mom says as she sits down with me on the couch, putting on a voice. She pats my thigh. Her big ring, my torn jeans.

"Kind of dull."

"Laura's bringing Bryan tonight."

"Who's Bryan?"

"Her new beau."

"Is he in TV?"

"No. I don't know. Maybe, I didn't ask."

"Tell him the CBC sucks ass."

"Mark!"

We hear Dad coming down the stairs, moving slow, and we stop, as he stops.

We hear him going back up the stairs, slowly.

"When are we eating?"

"When Laura gets here. How's the house?"

"Fine."

"Keeping it clean? Has Perry learned to cook yet?"

"He's learned to fry. He fries everything. I've never seen him cook anything unfried." She laughs.

I thought I was done but maybe I am still a bit hungover, sticky thoughts, creosote gumming up the pathways.

"Did you take him back to the doctor?" I ask.

"You and Bella were always so messy."

"You made us share a room."

"That's not why," she says, getting up.

I could go up to his study to check email but he might be there. On the mantelpiece, above the fireplace, there's a photo of the five of us in Spain. I was a kid. Laura was already a problem to herself. You can see it in her mouth. Dad's pacing about above me, clump clump. A few months before the park ranger took that photo Dad moved out for six weeks, coming and going. He told me then it was because he was very busy with work and I believed him, I actually forgot about it for years.

The doorbell rings and the door opens and Mom says ooh and goes, "Hi hi, give me your coat, hello dear, nice to meet you at last." I am picturing a redhead with freckles.

A few months ago it struck me, like fully: Dad moved out, he came back. Or was it that he spent two months in bed? I'm not sure what's true now and what I've dreamed. Bella doesn't remember and I can't ask Laura and Mom is not exactly neutral.

This guy Laura's brought with her is overeager. He says his full name every time he shakes hands. He looks young, but he's balding, keeps telling us all how much he's heard about us. I'm thinking lamb to the slaughter. He can't take his eyes off Bella's bright nostril stud.

Through the window dusk is coming, the trees are wrapping themselves up for it. I would like to go to sleep myself. Dad'll come down for dinner. Bryan is talking about their vacation. I thought they just met.

"I always, always wanted to go to Havana," says Mom, making him welcome. "But we never did." She adds that she loves Laura's necklace. Large amber stones on her black dress like medals she's won for sticking this out, for coming back to this.

"I thought you went to a resort," says Bella from the soft yellow chair.

"Yeah, it was so beautiful. You should go."

Bella's expression now.

"Sorry we were so late," says Laura. "I couldn't get away from work. We're putting together a new show, a new magazine."

"I'm going to turn down the chicken," says Mom and goes. I look over at Bella but catch Bryan's eye and he leans forward like he's got his script ready in his two hands. Fuck.

"So Laura tells me you're taking English. Do you know what you're going to do?"

"It's philosophy, actually," Bella says.

"Politics," I say.

"Have you thought about advertising? Great industry. Great people. Go places."

"The boy needs a plan," says my dad from the doorway.

I've been reading Hume this week: "On the Standard of Taste." And Hucket's *Technic*. He says we don't have selves. Apparently he got this from a Jesuit who travelled the world and learned it from a Buddhist. Well wouldn't that be awesome.

"Has he thought about advertising?"

"He needs direction."

"You know who had direction," I say over my shoulder to Dad.

"Who?"

"Stalin."

"Good," he laughs. "Good."

He and Bryan shake hands. I think Dad's about to fall.

"Have you thought about web design?" Bryan says to me as we stand up. "Growth industry. Especially now."

Dad has a cut on his hand that isn't healing.

Mom calls us and we're on the way into the kitchen.

Bella pulls at my big fuzzy sweater.

"How was Charlie's birthday?" she asks me.

"He wants to join the air force."

"What? Why? All your friends are such dicks."

"That's all I got out of him."

"Does he remind you of Christian Slater?" she whispers.

"Charlie?"

74

"No, Bryan."

"Bryan Grolier? No."

"His voice." She pulls me back again. "Hey. Hey. Why are you so quiet?"

"I'm not. Nothing."

Bella and I knew for sure we were foundlings when we were kids. Laura might be Mom and Dad's but we weren't. We'd hide from the people across the street, we were terrified of the sick. We had our own story. We had our own world.

Six of us around this familiar table now, starting to sit. Bryan telling Dad about the Mars mission. Maybe I am a bit more hungover than I thought. The mescal was a mistake. It always is. Let alone the main event, Charlie's Serbian mushrooms.

Mom brings over the salad from the counter in an elaborate bowl after checking everyone has plates. "We're very informal here," she says to Bryan, but she isn't. She's recently discovered beets and she's putting them into everything. "I found this salad in a book my lovely kids gave me," she says above the bowl. "The new Franco Morgan. Do you know him? Do you watch his show?" Bryan says he's heard of him. She's serving people and we pass the plates along. So everyone ends up with a different plate from what they started with. The portions get smaller as she goes until she comes to her own, she insists on serving herself last, and she only fills half her plate. There's none left and Bella takes the bowl back to the counter to make space. Dad's already started.

"Mark, you eat so much," says Mom. "Do you eat, during the week?"

"No," I tell her. "Do you want some of mine?"

"Aren't you hungry?"

"No, I am," I say, to reassure her. I'm not. Last night I was looking at leaves in the park, and they moved of their own accord, they danced.

Bella smiles and leans closer to me. "Mark, did you see it on Friday?" No one else is talking yet so they all hear. "I love it when he's in the dog suit and he pulls the car over."

"And everyone's naked in it."

"And everyone's naked!"

We're laughing.

"What are you discussing?" says Dad.

"Just this show we like."

"'I'm sure there's a rational explanation for this, officer,'" I say to Bella, and she cracks up.

"Have you seen their URL?" says Bryan.

I guess someone should engage him, but when I turn my head his way things spin. Mescal, mescalito. Psilocybin.

"It's got clips, scripts. Info."

"Cool."

"I'm sure there's a rational explanation," says Bella.

"That was great work last night," says Dad to Laura.

"Thank you."

"No really."

"Thanks Dad," she says, cautious.

"Phenomenal. The way you pronounced Herzegovina. The way you listened to that chap's report from Saskatoon. Really sensitive."

She's looking down into her plate. We all know that face.

"The way you said 'Kirby report.' Damn near brought a tear to my eye." Everyone's quiet because of his voice. "She gets paid a hundred thousand bucks a year," he says to the table. "To spout this stuff. Amazing. My daughter," he says, too loud, arm out.

"Simon," says Mom to Bryan, in a kind tone. "Do you work in TV, too?"

"No, I'm in web design," says Bryan, after a pause.

"What?" says Dad.

"Web design?"

Dad concentrates on the walnuts in his salad, the pumpkin seeds. The beets he's pushed to one side.

"For advertising companies mostly." Clink and scrape of tines on plates. "They do it all out of house these days."

"Are you still running, son?" Dad says to me.

"Did my 10K this afternoon," I tell him.

"And you're still single?"

"Yep."

He snorts. "Find yourself a nice divorcee."

And it passes.

Last night I wondered if the shape of my brain could still change, and I thought it could, it was happening as I thought the thoughts, that it hadn't been like this too long already. You always know what Mom and Dad are going to say.

Mom asks Laura to help her get the food from the oven. The kitchen's part of the room we're eating in, all open plan, like one big room. For a long time Mom wouldn't let Laura in the kitchen, when she first came back. Chicken mostly but potatoes, sprouts, nothing exciting, somehow the heartiness of it is tempting. Maybe I'm just tired. Maybe I'm mad, like them. Maybe I've damaged my brain badly. The dish comes to the table between her bright yellow soft oven gloves. Everyone aahs.

"I can't believe this," says Bella.

"Bella is a vegetarian, Bryan, so that's why we're not having lamb as I'd planned."

"I don't eat meat," Bella insists. "I told you I'm vegan."

"But what *is* that?" Mom asks, helpless.

"More Culo del Toro, Bryan?" Dad asks, proffering the bottle, winking at me.

"Bella, it's just chicken," says Mom.

"Sure, thanks."

"Pass me your glass."

"It won't kill you this one time," Laura says.

"Basically you don't give a shit, do you," says Bella, getting up and going to the fridge.

"Oh, don't do that darling," calls Mom.

The microwave door bangs shut.

"I'll make you an omelette."

"Mom!"

"What's she making?" Laura says to me. I'm looking at Bella over my shoulder.

"I have some tofu," she says.

"Sit down, Helène," says Dad. "If she wants to poison herself, let her. Save us the trouble."

"It's delicious," says Bryan, chewing.

I nod with my mouth full.

I woke up with my tongue burnt and went and sat in the park for a couple of hours, letting the sun warm me, getting hungrier and hungrier. I guess Bella was here, unless she crashed at a friend's. I wonder how breakfast was. Mom and Dad were here. Laura and Bryan slept over at her place or at his place, then they went shopping in the afternoon, I bet you anything. They went out for brunch.

Last night Suri and Richard got back together. We were sitting on the hill on the benches that look out over her neighbourhood. They were behind us and whenever we looked back, they were closer and closer, in conversation, until finally he had his arm around her, big relieved grins as if they'd got through a bombardment. Luckily I had a half-bottle of vodka in my bag. We went over and offered it to them to sort of celebrate only no one said that, we just looked at the turquoise light spreading between the houses, fingering the hedgerows. Every song in my head was the saddest song I'd ever heard but I could only remember about half of any of them. I was drunk. I was alone. I was coming down. My hands still didn't feel like my hands.

It's strange to take a piss in the middle of eating and I know it bothers Mom, but sometimes you have to. This is the last drop though.

Bella asked me if I'd finished my short story about the angry robots. Or the one about the oedipal brothers playing snooker. That's when I stood up.

When I come back Dad's telling Bryan about the plant. "Every chance the union got —" he says.

"They bled us," I finish for him.

"Exactly," he says. I sit again. "Any time we wanted to do anything, implement ... well ... anything. Stop. New regulations. New working conditions." He's braying now.

"Like what exactly?" says Bella.

"As if they didn't realize they were only leaving themselves in the shit. Putting the business in danger. They couldn't think it through." He slaps his liney white forehead.

"Pity the poor capitalist," says Bella.

"Last time I checked I was putting you through school."

Bella: "I think it's disgusting."

"Wait till you get to know the world," he says.

"What's disgusting?" asks Mom, concerned.

"I know the world pretty well," Bella continues, and she sounds confident.

"Do you really think," says Laura, "that you can alleviate poverty and hunger by taking a lot of acid?"

"No one's done acid in years," Bella scoffs. "What planet are you on?"

I laugh, too loudly. I shut up shop again.

"You don't know anything," says Dad. "Any of you."

"The world is fucked," says Bella, pointing her fork at him every other word. "My world. You think it's fine. As long as we've got our TVs."

"Bella," says Mom.

"Now I'm a slaveowner," says Dad.

"The only thing we talk about is what we like and what we don't. I like this. I don't like that. It's literally all we talk about! Don't you think there's anything else?"

"We're cows," says Dad. "We're pigs. Oh no, because you like those."

"Oh Joe," says Mom.

"I just learned that ninety percent of birds on this planet are poultry. Raised for us to eat. You like birds. You like watching them. You think that's right? You think that's okay?"

"Bella," says Mom, touching her hand and withdrawing. "Do you think you could try not to swear, dear?"

"That would imply some respect," Dad starts.

"If I were a dog or a horse or a fish —"

It's like she doesn't want to be conscious, I think. I get it.

"You didn't mind calling me to bail you out, did you?"

"Were you in prison?" says Bryan.

"I wasn't in prison," Bella says. "You didn't bail me out. I wasn't charged with anything. They pick you up, put you in holding for six hours and then let you go. To get you off the street and shut you up. There was an elevator down to the cells, just me and these two giant policemen, they took us down one at a time. Crowded House playing over the speakers. I was lucky because I was in a group of all girls. Josh got the shit beaten out of him."

But look, she smiles in the corners of her mouth when she talks about it.

"Was it dark?" I ask.

She stares at me like I'm an idiot.

"Are you like a real anarchist or something?" says Bryan.

"Bella is an activist," says Mom, pleased to have the word.

"Lock them up and throw away the key, I say," says Dad.

Mom mouths something but Dad's still talking.

"When Bella was little she had to write an essay on the poor. It started 'Once there was a very poor family. Everyone in the family was poor. The father was poor, the mother was poor.' She didn't know what to say next. 'The children were poor, the dog was poor, the cat was poor.' Didn't know what to say next. 'The maids were poor, the cook was poor, the gardener was poor. Even the chauffeur was poor.' That was her essay. That's Bella."

Bryan laughs. The rest of us, we've all heard the story. We hear it every Sunday. It was actually his essay.

"That's how you want to spend your time on this planet. Stuffing your face. You're not well!"

Mom is looking at Bella but it doesn't make any difference. Their eyes are the same; their eyes are rimmed red. I want this to stop.

"You're not yourself," Bella says. "You used to be different. You used to care. Who are you?"

Her face is red, like when we were kids, and she cried and cried and no one came. No one but me, but that's just because I was already there.

"You'd shoot us all," Dad says, cold. "In good time. And I'd be standing there against the wall. My heart full of love for you still. Overflowing."

I lift my wineglass to drink but for the second time it's empty.

We're eating dessert. People are chatting. Bryan's talking about whether it's easy for freelancers to get work in advertising or not. He says it is and then he says it isn't. Laura catches my eye to stop us every time he says anything Bella and me could make into a joke, but I know Bella's storing up his phrases. Next time she'll wear a T-shirt embossed with them. But I'm listening to the TV no one turned off as well as the conversation. It's dark outside, lights at the top of the houses across the street. Gardens. It's dark at four.

"Laura never really liked it here, did she —" I can imagine trying to bring it up with Mom. I try out different phrasings. We moved in and Laura left, came back six months later but even living here she wasn't really living here. She was in a kind of halfway house for three months, not an institution. We don't talk about it. When we visited her she was like one of the stuffed animals on her bed. She makes such an effort now it's embarrassing. I can think about it while eating cake. She hasn't mentioned it on her show yet. I wonder how much Bryan knows. Mom, could I have what she had? Is it passed down?

Then Dad. "Your mother and I have something to tell you. No stay, I don't want anyone to be uncomfortable. The situation is this. There is no money. Nothing left to pass on."

"Can I have the berries, Bry?"

"I always tried to be a good father. I thought I'd have something to leave you. I always thought I would leave a concrete legacy. But it is not so."

"I always tried to be pompous," says Laura.

"Laura!" Bella chirps, feigning shock. "What a bad, unloving daughter!"

"We have to sell the house, and your mother will move in with one of you. The cottage too of course. We've spoken to the … the steward? The agent. It is all in train."

Mom says his name.

"I will go," he says. "I won't be a bother to you."

Again.

"There is nothing. It is all gone. I hope you will feel able to make your peace with me. For I must make my peace with God."

"There's no God, Dad," says Bella.

"We established that last week, I think," Laura says.

He closes his eyes and raises his hands to his face. Mom crosses herself. Bella chooses this moment to ask Bryan with her eyes for the red. Bryan doesn't know what to do.

"With God," Dad says, but you can barely hear him.

"It's all right, Dad," I say.

Everything's quiet.

"Hey, listen, there are steps you can take," says Bryan. "My friend knows a really good family lawyer, they went through something similar because it's not uncommon and I'm sure he can take you through some —" Only then Laura rests her hand gently on his.

The first time Dad made the speech we thought it was true. We argued for hours. Then Laura looked in his desk and from what she could tell, the house was safe, the pension was working, everything was paid for. We called his lawyer and his accountant, and they were mystified. Every so often he says it again, though, as if for the first time. He's not well. But we don't talk about it. We let it go. It's familiar. Pretty soon he'll be complaining about the Habs again.

"Would anyone like coffee?" says Mom. "Tea?"

Then very quickly everyone's standing, piling up plates, forking leftovers into the bin. Bella stops me by the fridge, whispers. "What is it? Did she dump you again? Nasty mean Sonia. Sorry."

"Bella."

It was Annie this time. And it's more like she never came back.

"You find this all so annoying, don't you," she says. "It's childish."

I am not loved.

"I'm tired is all."

"What did you say?"

I am not heartbroken.

"Is it because of your big fuzzy sweater?"

Last night there was a girl I'd taken art history with, but she wasn't interested. That Eva girl was there too, and another time I saw her at Skeme. I saw her at Milk. This rich Austrian was talking about getting caught speeding on his motorbike. Three hundred schilling, he was saying, that's a lot of money. For me, too, he said, as if someone had objected.

"I just drank too much last night," I tell her. "That's all. You have any shows coming up?"

"It's your armour. You put it on to come into this house," she says.

"And you don't?"

"You don't have to say anything," says Bella, her eyes huge, holding both my hands in hers. "Not to me."

Then Mom's talking about port. Maybe the game's on. Dad and Bryan go upstairs for Bryan to show Dad how to work something on the computer. "We could all go for a lovely neighbourhood walk," says Mom, but it's dark. Bella picks up the phone and takes it into the family room and you can hear her immediately making plans for tonight. I'm standing by the kitchen door trying to think if anyone will see me go out front for a smoke. Mom and Laura putting away the dishes. I don't think they notice me.

"I had to go to the pharmacy last weekend and it was almost impossible. It was like Soviet Russia trying to find a place that was open. When we moved back here from London, everything was closed on Sundays. No bars no restaurants no theatre. You don't know." Hands Laura the bowl. "You don't remember. Like when we used to try and find a restaurant open after your violin recitals. How would you remember? We were at a show."

"I remember we'd go to McDonald's. Why didn't you just hit Shoppers?"

"It was after the theatre. Your father wanted to see a show."

Do I even have my lighter on me? Pockets. Jacket.

"I hate driving downtown, and a police car pulled us over. I'd had a little too much to drink. But luckily it was a lady policeman."

Mom covers her mouth in the dishcloth.

"But just as she was asking us where we'd been she got a call on her radio and rushed back to her police car. I drove away!"

"You did what? Mom, that's really dangerous."

"She didn't follow us. They really don't, you know," Mom says, behind green and white stripes, pretending to be know-ledgeable.

86

Laura's hands are at her sides now, she's turned to face her. "Why did you do that, Mom?"

"I like Bryan. He's charming."

"What's with you all?"

"What?"

"I just drove away," Mom says. "I didn't want to spoil the evening."

But Laura's laughing a little.

"You're all nuts," says Laura, watching me from out of the corner of her eye. "We're all running."

Mom says, "My father always wanted to be an actor, you know. Your grandfather."

"I know," Laura says.

I go out with smokes and try to think things through. Sit on the porch in the light rain, can't see the sky. Maybe Dad'll come out at some point. His light's on above me, up there. He's with Bryan.

If there was someone I'd get home and give her a call and she'd come over and ask me how dinner was. We'd smoke up. She'd throw a pebble at my window.

That's the other thing about hangovers. You get so fucking maudlin.

A WHOLE
FRESH
CARAPACE

Carapaces-tobella.doc

A WHOLE FRESH CARAPACE **good title**
by Mark Ferguson-Cohane
that what you're calling yourself now?

Sometimes he woke up before the suit did and lay as quiet
and still as he could, so as not to wake it, listening to himself, his self, breathing in and out beneath the iron runnels. It
seemed like being awake was a continuation of his dream of
flight. Of course the suit eventually detected the change in
his breathing, the gradual rise in body temperature, and all
its functionalities kicked in one by one. But he would carry
around a moment like that for days, secretly, like a girl's name.
Morning after morning his suit raised him, servos grinding,
the accordion-like fauld already contracting at his belly, the
whirr of bolts in the cowter. And he began to wonder: these
moments, when I wake up, when I lie here inside this thing that
is me — are *these* dreams of another life?

91

*

Bodies clanked against bodies on the train, snapping Robby from his reveries. There was no space, no time. And then he followed all the other great cylindrical metal legs up the dusty wet smudged black steps out of the station. For the walk to work he always listened to music as loud as he could set it, but it was never loud enough. Down in the undersea taverns one night a friend from his old school had told him the system could be hacked, that the speakers in his great helm could go much louder, and he wanted to give that a try.

He could see her ahead of him, like every morning. He'd started trying to catch ~~a~~ **this** particular train every morning, because often it arrived at the same time as her bus. He knew the number painted on her pauldron, 00673A. The screen on her casque showed a pair of green eyes, **what is this from?** gleam-ing. Before, he'd seen her walking from the station with a boy in lilac tactical gear, but this whole week she'd been alone. She's broken up with him, he thought, he's on a different work rota, he's gone on vacation, he'll be back tomorrow. They worked in different units in the plant and she always shone and he'd never spoken to her and she'd never noticed him. The fact that they worked in the same place had changed — he wasn't sure when — from the perfect excuse to talk to her into the perfect reason not to. He swallowed so grimly that his gard-brace clunked. He checked his greaves again, making sure he was all still there; thieves were rampant these days.
part of me goes oh dear here like all very teenage obsessive silent unrequited loving you know? "Underneath I'm Different" sorry sweetie

When he'd started working at the plant four months before, the goal of polishing a thousand electro-knuckles a day had seemed fantasy; but now he found he had to pace himself not to reach it, lest Ulrich set him a higher quota. A knuckle or a halberd or an escutcheon came off the conveyor at his left and he had to pick it up, squirt compressed air at it, spray it with the fluid and then pull his turquoise cloth through, then hold it under the lamp where it turned blue if it passed or red if it was defective. He either put it on the belt to his right or dropped it into the yellow bin at his feet. **Who cares** Sometimes his mind could wander — to **OO673A for consistency OK?**, to various scenes in which they were alone, and she was unscrewing nozzle B at his waist, to his music, but the problem was that he had to pay just enough attention — picking up the air cannister, getting the spray in the right place at the right pressure — that, though he didn't have any interest in what he was doing, his mind needed to be involved for ~~him~~ **his body** to avoid mistakes. That was torture.

When the bell sounded he hid under the storeroom stairs until the security guards, singing out to each other, finished their cursory checks. Then before the cleaning staff rolled in he got down to his important business **too explainy, I want it to be a dream, and there's no voiceover in dreams, no narrating — it just happens. I feel like you're marching on stage to tell me what's what. Let it happen —** He held a black bag in his left gauntlet and with his right he was rooting through wires and metal rings, looking for anything that he could sell or use. One time in the flushing department he'd found an entire plackart and bought a set of turntables with the proceeds. It was amazing what people found defective, and what others were willing to pay for it on the street, given the shortages. As he bent, steam escaped from the perforations at his knee.

He laughed, down awkwardly on all fours, gripping the blue trashcan neck with one hand, other arm in it down to the shoulder. He'd found part of a hauberk. Then he had the knowledge that he was being watched and he froze. There was the click and scratch of metal, a metal bird uncrossing enormous wings. Without moving he tried to soften himself for the security guard's mattock to the head. But he tensed again when nothing came. He looked to the right, fractionally, just enough to see a number disappearing out of the wooden warehouse door. **0673B as prev.** The *kiss me kiss me kiss me* of her sollerets clacking on the tiled floor died away eventually. **Nice. Pure dopamine, this sentence: I'm looking out of the window at the squirrels feeling it**

*

He had tried to tell his mother what it was like for him. He couldn't explain it very well. They'd end up fighting, and he'd go up to his room or crash out into the street to meet his friends. He wanted to tell her he felt that there was something *on* him. She might have felt it once, he thought. But all she heard, as far as he could tell, was her boy going off the rails, even getting close to the terrorist sloganeering. And he saw how ~~how~~ her screen misted in her fear. She told him to be quiet and went back to making him his dinner, arranging and rearranging silver serving bowls of a good size, steam pouring from the sink the whole entire time. **Lots of steam here. Is rust a problem?**

"Don't you get tired of it?" he said to her rubbed spaulders.

She didn't even understand what he meant.

"Look," he said, "Look." He pulled at his gorget to show her the underskin underneath, the white flesh with little black hairs. He'd seen it, just for a second, experimenting one night in his room.

Mom wouldn't like any of this. and yeah this whole part's a little flat. This Story is about him, not mom. But I mean the language too: all over it's a little too correct. (like your old brothers and the snooker table story). Like an essay for school not a story. I mean, what if you stick twenty thousand volts in and see what happens!!! Let yourself cut loose. (and all the armour words are just weird --lose some).

"Be careful!" she screamed, "The air!"

"You don't believe that, do you?"

"For God's sake," she told him, "Why are you doing this to yourself?"

"It's all bullshit, Mom," he said.

"Who are you talking to, Robby?" she asked. "Is it someone at the plant?"

There's more to me, he thought that night, than this thing you see. Much more. It's normal to you, he thought lying on his bed. Not me. You don't know me at all, do you. Because underneath this, I'm different. **TOLD YOU!!!**

She clattered into his room as if she'd been listening to his thoughts.

"You think there's something else inside of you?" she shrieked. "This is you! This is what you are. This!" She clanged her spatula against his plackart. "This!"

*

Rumours battled rumours. It was the atmosphere he'd grown up in. Robby didn't say much, but he listened intently. He sat at the corner seat at one of the long tables in the courtyard — in the summer they let them outside at lunch — with some of the older workers, men who'd been at the plant twenty or thirty years. He liked the passionate arguments they had about the most insubstantial trivia; he liked their fantastic crudeness when they talked about female colleagues. **I guess there's an inevitablity to this but I _don't like_ it** Shortly after starting work there he'd let it be known that he could secure them any kind of narcotic, **you naughty boy** and that had made him, if not popular, at least a tolerable novelty. For himself, Robby found that drugs, some drugs at least, loosened the tight bolts at his collarbone and cuirass, gave him the feeling of lightness he'd dreamed about. Though the next morning the onion breath killed him, and he felt twice as clamped down as before. **Yup**

Today Anderson was sombre and barely spoke above an amplified whisper, head sunk into his reddy brown breastplate of distressed iron, so that his crest rather than his screen angled towards them. When finally they'd exhausted all other topics of conversation and almost all their extended cigarettes and were sitting in silence, Brandywine cleared his throat and

96

asked Anderson what in goddamn hell was fucking wrong with him. Anderson's neck motors whirred as he lifted his head up and groaned as he dropped it again. He paused. Then he spoke:

"There was a girl on the train today. On the platform at any rate. We were all waiting for the 7:40, everyone minding his own business, everyone just looking at his own sabatons, and she suddenly starts screaming. Pretty thing, leather cover around her fauld. I'd noticed her out of the corner of my eye." They all roared knowing laughter. "No, not like that." He continued sadly. "Like she could be my daughter." The laughter died away. "And then she starts screaming, and I look around. I go over to help her, I thought maybe her life support had given out and someone's hit the station emergency and a klaxon goes off and then I see what she's doing. She's yelling 'You don't need to wear these things.' **Rpt** Part of me says: What things? But I knew what she meant. She's ripping at herself, pulling bits off herself." **Your armour = your big fuzzy sweater!?!?**

They were all silent. This wasn't a wise thing to be talking about.

"'The real you is under it,' she screams. 'The truth's underneath.'"

"What does that mean?" Ulrich scoffed.

"Did she start burning up?" Jones asked.

"What happened?" Robby said intently.

Anderson looked surprised, as if he hadn't expected to tell them all this. He spoke quickly and quietly, like a hurried mechanic. **Isn't that what he is?** "Well out of nowhere there was a squad, and they gave her a whack in the helm, and that shut her down, and then they wrapped her in a rubber cloth and carried her away like a carpet. Nothing to see here, ladies and germs."

"Serve her right," said Brandywine, starting to gather up his lunch straw and then stopping. **Mrs Davies always taught us, a period at the end of a sentence.**

"Did she really start burning up, though?" asked Robby. "Was she coughing up the poison or was she fine?"

Anderson spoke dreamily, as if he hadn't heard him.

"I was thinking, what does a pretty young thing like her go and destroy herself for? Whole life before her and ... she was so thin. And so angry." **Always Her Body: You could go down the wrong path here.**

"Guerilla," Ulrich said. "Redblack. We should report you. Snake." They all laughed nervously. Ulrich went on in a milder but still definitive tone. "But really there's no such thing as a ~~snake~~ **Snake**. There are no ~~redblacks~~ **Redblacks**. There are no guerrillas, just thieves. They reel people in: old romantics like you, Tom — yes like you Tom, you're an old whore, don't deny it. Then they cut you up for scrap and leave you for dead." **Hmm. Interesting.**

"But why would she do that?" Robby interjected ~~but some-one else was talking.~~

"I heard," Brandywine **(Brandywine?! Too weird. Change name)** began from under his immense casque, "That they take off their skins to show you an underskin — soft and smooth like," they all made a noise between a hum and a sigh. "They show it you, lull you in. Like in the olden days. You can't resist. But it's all fake. Their real body is underneath that wet rubber.

But meanwhile you're burning up in the atmosphere, and they're laughing. You know what a whole fresh carapace gets you in the alleys today?" **yuck**

I keep waiting for Dad to walk in and tell them all to get back to work. It feels like you're tyring to say you're too clever for this company, which isn't the best, but okay, I get it

Robby was thinking, Like in the olden days?

The gong went and they all stood up with metallic squeals, except for him. His mind was disturbed and speeding. He only woke up when he felt rather than saw someone standing directly to his right, the gleaming borders of two dark encrusted gauntlets catching the light at the table's edge like a promise. **Nice**

"My name's Sonia," she said.

Come on Mark change her name at least.

I mean how many times is this girl going to break up with you? sorry

*

Walking along the artificial beach together, with the artificial waves throwing artificial spume at the artificial sand, walking along amongst the other metal couples, gauntlet in gauntlet. Sunday afternoon — and he knew, even as he was having the experience, that he would not forget this day, this bliss.

"Rust kills," an advertising voice boomed out in their heads.

Suddenly she ran away from him up into the dunes. He gave chase; he found her lying in a hollow on the other side of the second dune. They could hear the people clink and coo but they could not be seen. The sun glinted off her vambraces. It was hot, even with his temperature moderator on full blast.

"What have you done to me?" he said.

"It's what you've done to me," she answered.

He had never experienced this — this need to be with her at all times, the flares of delight so powerful he could barely stand through them, the desperation when she was gone. She had taught him about old books, and giant's fossils, ~~about~~ **and** soft and supple things **(fossils = hard)**. She said it was all still there in the world, you just had to look, you just had to dig. She said his fears about the toxic air were just paranoia. She was fierce in her self-belief. She said it was nothing to do with the Government, it was just up to the two of them. It's up to you to be free, she said. To take flight. **My prediction: manic pixie dream girl is going to chop your nuts off at the end. Haha. Sorry.**

He wanted to show her the real him. Not the clunky Robby the world saw, but the person he really was. Not this metal thing — he felt its weight now. He wanted to share something with her — nozzle to nozzle, depth to depth. He wanted it to be possible. She was another world.

"I saw what you did," she said. "I see what you do. You could be useful," she said, "to the right people. You're a regular little gangster, aren't you?"

Robby thought his temperature rise might be obvious.

"I wanted to show you something," she said. She propped herself up on her sharp elbow cowters to make sure no-one was coming. Her hinges hummed as she bent towards her stretched out schynbalds. **What the fuck is a schynbald? Someone has**

to read this, right? From somewhere she had produced a tiny green electric screwdriver. "Look," she said.

She worked at the screws on the bottom of her poleyn and then focused on the greave. She had to pull at it first, with some force, and unplug some delicate red wires. "Remember where those go," she said in a sardonic tone. Then she snapped the guard off and he saw, astounded, the calf beneath. Pink and soft and tender, the very opposite of him. He wanted to touch. "It's you," he said. "You're like vellum." **I am dancing around my room singing "And I am KINKY!"**

"Yes."

"Beneath," he knocked on his breastplate.

"Yes."

"Really you."

There was a drawing on her underskin. He'd thought it was a coloured circle. Now he saw a curled-up snake made up of red and black triangles, eating its own tail.

"It doesn't hurt? You're not burning up?"

"Look at me."

For a moment he did just look, and then something pulsed in him and he reached out and touched her soft underskin, the balloon of soft relaxed muscle behind her shin. And touching it with his ironclad knuckles he looked up at her, so moved he hardly trusted his voice.

"I want you to see me," he said. "I want to be rid of this thing."

"You can be."

"I think you're the only person who understands," he whispered, and courageous, he pulled her sallet gently towards his grille.

"No," she told him gently. "We're a movement, Robby. And all this," she added, "It's going to be torn away. You can be part of it. But I don't know how much to say. I need to know you can be trusted."

Is the activism supposed to be me? Thanks. Do you think things can go on the way they are? Do you even want that? Or the environment. Do you have any social OK rant over

"Yes," he said. "It's what I want."

"I'll be honest with you, Robby. Not everyone survives it. Not everyone can take it. There's a lot of comfort in the suit. You can walk away now."

"I can take it," Robby said.

"I thought you'd say that," Sonia whispered, and her rondel clunked against his ventail, then scratched, and the noise echoed like the sea around them. "I used to think I was alone in here. It was a big thing for me, to learn I wasn't alone. There are many of us, Robby. Do you want it though? To be part of something?"

"I dreamed of you before we met," he told her, groaning. "I dreamed of this."

"I want to see your face," she said hungrily, ~~while~~ just touching at his nozzle B.

*

I forgot to say I do like how you break things up with stars
She said she had to make some calls. She said she had to make some preparations. So it was a week later he went to her place. He'd brought a garbage bag that was so full of elbow cops,

wings, and rivets that it talked when he moved. It was a plain apartment on the second floor of a Victorian house. Her room-mates were all out, she said. There was white paint over parts of the floors. The cell would meet them, she said. They could get started, in the meantime, she said, if he wanted to. They had a little time. He nodded.

I feel like a little atmosphere would help – is it raining? Smell of fish and chips hanging in the air? Because it does all feel like England somehow. Why not Little Portugal? And what does she look like, by the way? A cylon?

With a great shimmy she banged her tasset against a panel in the wall and a keyboard dropped down. She wired him up and he lay on the bed as instructed, feeling a little numb now, feeling quiet.

"What are you doing?"

"Just being safe. You've never done this before."

"You mean the air?"

"I mean the shock."

He watched her type, thinking.

"So how many times have you?" he asked her, trying to make it sound like he was just asking, but he went on, not giving her the chance to answer. "When are they coming? The rest of them."

"Soon," he heard. "And it never meant anything. Not like this."

She leaned over him and pressed at the edges of his cuirass. She hit a few more keys and he felt warmth in his upper parts. He was nervous all of a sudden, but he didn't want to look cowardly in front of her, he didn't want to disappoint her. He couldn't back out now, though he suddenly wondered, Why was this so important to me?, as if he were cold, as if he were someone else.

"Won't my alarm go off?" he said.

"I can deal," she told him.

"So when are they coming?" he asked again.

As the warmth grew, he felt her gingerly lift his chest plate off. He saw his underskin, the biggest tranche of it he had ever seen. It was very white, and looked **puffy and** damp. It had been bunched under the metal so long that the lines and curves impressed into it had become part of its fabric. He was amazed — elated somehow — by all the tiny beige hairs on his white body. He'd never known there were so many. It was like looking at a forest from the air, or taking the roof off a termite colony: he imagined there were civilizations there for her to discover and guide. He realized he felt no pain at all, no burning.

I don't get this, is it that she's drugged him somehow? Or is it that there's nothing to be scared of? Is htis about sex or politics? I know it's show don't tell but I want to know what's going on, you know?

"Take more off," he said.

She snapped off his vambraces and turned him round and carefully unbolted the pauldrons and rerebrace and in a few minutes his top half, between neck and waist, was exposed.

"The real me," he said.

"Do you want me to?" she asked. Of course he nodded. It was easier for her, with her experience. And he noticed, with a touch of disappointment, now that he was watching it come off, that her body looked cobbled together. Up close he could see that it came from different sources, it was a jumble of different makes; surely it could barely function. He wondered how it was he'd never noticed before. She dropped herself down in a pile piece by piece. His parts she'd carefully arranged.

She was bigger than him. She was wide and spacious, and it made him feel more like a child than he wanted to; it looked as if another girl could fit within her. But he shrugged that off. He was thinking, This is something no one else has seen. This is as close as it's possible to get. This is real, at last, this is real.

Calmly, professionally, she went to work on his tasset, fauld, and cuisses. Then as in his dreams she dropped her aegis to the floor.

This reminds me of that time you said the seven most beautiful words in the English language were And then she took her top off. I mean, girls read stories too, Mark. Womyn. Just sayin.

*

He woke up sweating, feeling soft and wet and unfamiliar to himself. The bed was empty next to him and the mattress was damp. He thought he heard steps in the hall: the noise had woken him. He was falling asleep again when he heard a clink of metal dropping to the floor and then a noise exactly like a barrel rolling down a ramp. Then there was a loud, brief sawing sound. "Sonia?" he called. Bleary, onion breathed. "Son?"

A quick high squeal. He propped himself up to call out better and felt weak and cold and thin and small and somehow ashamed. He pulled the sheet up to cover himself, but found it rubbed him harshly. Then he was looking around the room at the peeling wallpaper and improvised shelves — plywood planks resting on clay cylinders. He stood up, ~~looking~~ **reaching** desperately for his suit, but he heard only silence and then the sound of his lungs clawing at the air. His bag of goods was gone. **Oh no!**

He dropped the sheet and clutched at himself. Blue-white light in the room jutted in from the open naked window, where a million brick houses watched him. He thought he heard a siren. He wondered what time it was now.

"Mom," he said.

Sonia had piled up his suit at the bottom of the bed but there was just floor there now; there was no trace of hers, either. It was him, he was here, but how would he piss? How could he eat? Head spinning, struggling for breath, he didn't know where he was. He swallowed snot and it tasted thick and bloody.

"Mom?" he called again.

Robby stumbled out into the empty hall, the harsh wood scraping his feet. Maybe she was in the washroom, maybe she'd gone to get ice cream. Water came from his eyes and he hugged himself and saw that the house was incredibly bare. He wandered into the kitchen, and it was empty; how had he not seen this room? There weren't even drawers above the floor cabinets, just empty black rectangles. **Ok but why would there be drawers _above_ the cabinets?** There were no books.

He sneezed and the sneeze became a coughing fit and a scraping in his windpipe and there was nothing to cushion it, there was no help for him, and he hugged himself with his thin bare arms, hearing the sirens get louder, red spots and scars near his elbows, and then a siren impossibly loud. He was looking for a tablecloth. He was looking for cardboard. Anything.

Yes I feel the panic here. I feel like I want 00673A to come back for some payoff tho. Also, is she putting on his stuff or selling it? Doesn't she have access to the thrown away stuff too? AND If there's thrown away stuff, why does she need his parts??? Because htey're better? So many questions...

Frantic, he ran back to the bedroom as he heard a door downstairs crashing open and the sound of men's raised voices. He felt feverish and about to swoon. He stepped in something squishy, and he picked up the wet pieces of a huge, shapeless, rubbery piece of pink material, like the body of some unknown sea creature, ancient seahorse born of plastic waste **good**, by-product of pollution. He looked at it, at the drawing between his hands that he'd seen on her calf, a red and black circle, a snake. Then he started to cough, and he could not stop.

Marky Marky Mark
I feel like maybe I haven't said this enough to you: You're a good writer! This is all really sad and lonesome. It feels like 1984 meets Doctor Who and I like some of the images a lot. It hits home (maybe because I know you?)

NOW THE BEEF PATTY PART OF MY BURGER OF RESPONSE:
gotta say I'm confused at the end – so is she a guerilla?
I thought they weren't real, that she was a thief!! But then
she has the snake. So the mom and colleagues were right?
Also, how do the police know to come? (I thought that
was just the paranoia theme). Or maybe I'm just taking
it the wrong way, maybe you don't need to be so logical
with this kind of thing, you writers in your garrets...
Though a song has a shape too, that's where I'm coming
from. Sometimes I start with the second verse and work
backwards and forwards.

Because really what I feel is, don't take this the wrong
way, but what if you have this all wrong as a concept?
Everyone here is saying the same thing: our true self is
underneath all our armour and it's bad so keep it hidden
(mom) or it's good so set it free (apparent Sonia).

But what if that's wrong Mark? What if there's nothing
under the armour? That's kind of what I'm feeling these days:
things come, things go, but I don't know who I am, underneath. Maybe I'm just the things coming and going, telling
myself that there's more to me than that (and when we're
in pain because of what some person or other in our lives
has done to us our self feels so real, I know that, sweetie.)
I don't want to make it all about me but hey there's a reason
you sent me this Marky... isn't there?

That bigger question is somewhere under this story Mark.
It's the bigger more troubling question. And I think stories
need to be trouble.

But I don't know much. Maybe you've sent this out to the New Yroker and won a big writing prize already.

Anyway, thanks for sharing! Ha! See you Sunday night?

So many hugs and kisses and deepest love my dearly drippy brother

Bella Bella Bella

YOU GUYS

So this is last month: we've got to the point in the night when no one's looking at cards any more. Two guys are still in, but Charlie's on the Xbox, and Rich and Perry and me are talking, drinking. One eye on the table but we're not going to buy back in again and lose more money now. Pretty fucking late and sometime later I go down the hall to the can and there's a poster of Audrey Hepburn and I think fuck, since Heather moved in Ty's really fucking changed. Almost lose my balance but hold on to the shower curtain, it's like the ocean sideways, I think he didn't have that before. Something Audrey Hepburn brought with her when she moved in. Some of us have girlfriends, some of us live alone, Perry's married and he has a kid, I live alone. Three little fucking seashells on the cistern lid, Jesus Christ. My head spins for a sec. Messages on my phone. A product breakthrough I don't want to be thinking about. My sister's coming home.

The kitchen and the living room are one big room, Ron and Ty are still at the table, they're the serious card players, the four of us are talking — Charlie's got killed on Halo too many times — backs against the kitchen counter, Heineken Heineken Corona Schlitz. Fucking Charlie, can of Schlitz. Where did he even get it? He's talking about how there's this wind blowing in at work and he's going to get fired. He's in software, marketing. But these are good guys, good guys. It doesn't sound like it but we went down to New York, and all they wanted to do was shop, count celebrities. Perry tends bar, but he's a singer, got a band, *eye* called them the best unsigned talent in the city. He opened for Bella; Bella opened for him. There was moisturizer in the washroom, I saw it, that's okay. Tired. I'm telling Perry about how I've started thinking that ball games inherently suck compared to games of luck and chance, something I saw on the web, and I hear Charlie saying "I don't *want* to see a picture of you pissing on a girl. Rich, Jesus. You're such a fucking pervert. Jesus."

If we are drunk Richie is drunkest. He sways, pushes the phone up at Charlie's chin. Rich is short, he looks like a mound of something. Cauliflowers. But he's built. We did track for a while together. He always beat me into second.

"I'll fucking send it to you. I'm sending it to all of you."

His big thumbs podge the little buttons. Me and Perry have come closer because this conversation sounds better.

"Fucking sicko."

He looks at me like I'm gay or something.

Charlie: "Don't want to know, don't want to know, did I say I wanted to know?"

Rich looks up from his cell.

"You know how we're different Charles, you know how we're different? You're a pussy. You talk about it all the fucking time but you never do anything. But I do."

Perry asks them what they're talking about.

Richie turns his phone round, he's annoyed he has to start his story over.

Perry groans at the phone and laughs.

"I was in Florida for RPX. St. Petersburg. Big convention. All night I'm there at the bar with Terrence" — Charlie's brother, they both work for Horseman — "talking to girls, getting the cold shoulder. Finally dipshit wants to call it a night, so fine, we take the elevator up and on floor five these two girls come in, drunker than we are. Ten seconds to make a deal so I invite them up to our suite, and they say they work for fucking Seagram. Come to our suite. We've got a suitcase full of vodka coolers, amaretto, everything, in *their* room free because it's publicity."

He takes a drink.

I miss Annie so fucking much for a second. God.

"So we go. We're talking about Florida, how in ten years it's going to be underwater." He lowers his voice for one sentence but then it comes up again. "Things are just starting to get interesting when your limp-dick brother *excuses* himself and leaves. Which isn't cool."

"Terry told me his one was skanky. Dirty girl."

"Bullshit. Bull. Shit. Pussy."

"Okay, Rich."

I'm looking at the phone now. Rich's hairy belly and the shining girl's shining middle, midriff. His cock, seen from above, poking out of his fist. Didn't need to see that. Little eye blinking.

Perry says: "I'm going to have fucking nightmares man."

Charlie says: "Couldn't you have photoshopped yourself a bigger dick?"

"Gay. Anyway," says Rich, and then he's delicate all of a sudden: "My comrade at arms vacates the field. His girl says she's going back to the bar, forgot her purse, some bullshit. So we're on the bed." Whispers. "But I can't fuck her. I'm too fucking drunk by this point. I'm fucking her, I mean, of course, fuck, but I can't come. Too much beer, wine, vodka. She's rolling me around like a fish on the deck. I get her to come, of course, but I know I'm not going to. Like I'm too seasick. I'm seriously starting to feel like I'm going to puke on her or something."

Rich looks around to make sure it's only us he's telling.

Very quietly: "Anyway so I pull out, stand up, stand above her, I come this close to falling over and cracking my skull on the bedside table, the Bible. I go to the washroom and I'm standing there then I hold back, I think wait a minute. I come out, and she's on the bed squeezing her tits together and I say why not."

Now he's talking in this self-amazed tone, wide-eyed, and I don't know if it's something he's putting on, is he reeling us along, or is he genuinely amazed, is he hypnotized. Ty and Ron are listening now too, cards down on the table. There is music: iPod in the iDock. Emotional Rescue.

"So I stand next to her, and she turns her mouth towards me and I say no, just put a hand down to keep her there, and aim with my other hand" — he does the motions for us —

"I hold my cock, and I start to piss on her. I piss up and down her, and I tell you it's like fucking pissing and coming at once. And she's *writhing* and fucking loving it. It's like crack on your cock or something, it's like a schoolgirl's asshole, I have seriously never felt anything like this."

We're all shock and awed.

"Then I think fuck I've got to get this on tape and I get my phone from the floor; pissing on the carpet, fuck."

"I'm surprised she didn't just fucking stab you."

"Fuck man. She was writhing."

The sheets, I think: what about the sheets?

"Jesus fucking Christ Richie."

"Jesus Christ."

Rich says: "True story." The phone comes back to him, and he smiles at it like a dad at the playground.

Back there Ty flops his cards down on the table, says he's out.

Rich is married, the fucking guy's married.

Last night I drove out to Christina's mom's house. I've never been there, never met her mom and dad. I just thought sometimes you're going through things, and you want to talk, maybe it's even better if it's someone you don't know all that well. I'd run into Rich outside his work, and I took him for lunch because he looked like he'd been hit by a train. When we were holding the little menus I couldn't remember when I'd seen him except for poker nights the last few years. I mean never the two of us alone. But he talked enough for both of us. He told me Chris had moved out, she'd moved up to her mom's place in

North York, Bayview and Steeles. Up where there's a mosque next door to a synagogue next door to a Chinese temple, I said, Oh Canada. He said all three were gigantic. I didn't even say that much to him. I thought he was going to cry into his burrito. He hadn't shaved, the top of his collar was yellow, I said to him you've got to look after yourself, man. When I got back to the office I Canada 411d all the Petruccis in North York.

I didn't call or anything, but sometimes things work out, like sometimes you switch into the collectors on impulse and it's quicker than the express lanes. I was listening to a CD I burned five years ago. These houses on Rolson are ranchy, American. Some of them it looks like you took on too many projects: a way old Porsche on flat tires in the way of a sloping basketball hoop. But then you don't know, you might walk into a Sikh doctor's house or a Russian accountant's, you don't know up here. In the car I thought, I hope she doesn't think this is weird. I hope her mom doesn't answer the door. But it was Christina. The first moment I think she didn't recognize me: she was behind the mosquito mesh.

"Mark?" she said. She showed me in. She was wearing these grey track pants that just hung away from her butt, and her eyes were puffy, like she was crying just before, like she was rubbing it out of her eyes before she answered. But some women, it doesn't matter if they're dressed in a potato sack. She looked domestic, and I felt it was like she was my wife, like I was coming home to my wife, and she was welcoming me back from a hard day at the office, making me a drink. You're such an idiot, Richie, I thought. She asked if I wanted a coffee.

"What are you doing here, Mark?" she asked.

I asked how she was and she asked how I was, and she shrugged, and she said she was up and down. Then she laughed and said no, terrible, actually. She said she just got off the phone with him. She was about to say more, but then she stopped. She asked when we'd last seen each other and I said it was Perry and Lynn's dinner, their joint birthday thing. She said oh yeah, the fondue, and I nodded.

Christina's a teacher. She's a brunette, Italian I guess, although the name Christina doesn't sound Italian so I don't know. Ponytail, not bangs. She was wearing this brown fleece that looked comfy. She looked down and said she hadn't been expecting anyone, company. I told her it wasn't that Rich had asked me to come, I said I just wanted to see how she was doing, if she needed anything. If she needed some consoling I wasn't going to say no, of course. I'm happy to console. She probably hadn't shaved her legs since she moved out.

She talked a bit about living back here with her mom for the first time in so long, how that felt. The conversation before the Conversation. We could have been in a bar, I thought, not sitting on the two sides of the island in her mom's kitchen, sitting up on barstools like little kids home for lunch. I do miss my mom, I said. I wish my dad wasn't sick.

"You know what's going on, I guess."

I say I kind of know.

She gets up, she says she totally forgot, she goes over to the coffee maker, asks me how I like it. Now her voice is all serious, like she doesn't want to talk about her mom's cooking anymore.

"I thought Rich might mess around on me," she says all of a sudden. "But I thought it would be in twenty years, I could see him getting bored. Maybe then. Not now."

Then she breathes in quick, like she's just realized and it's got to her.

Looking down she says, "Someone sent me these pictures of Rich with..." She talks to the cupboards, in profile from me, she doesn't look at me. "It doesn't matter. I thought I could have dealt with — well no, I couldn't have dealt with it, things would have happened, what happened happened. But the pictures were so..."

She pauses.

"This is hard for me to talk about. And obviously it wasn't just his dirty secret. Other people knew. So what are you going to do."

I wonder if I should have made the coffee, instead of her making it for me. She looks exhausted. I get up from my stool and go round the island over to her. She's shaking, but when I get close she freezes up. She's crying, and I give her my consolation hug, her hair smells dirty and strong. She starts shaking again. I move my hand down her back, nowhere dangerous, just testing, and she's stiff.

"We were trying for a baby," she says in a dead voice.

"I know," I say, "I know."

"You know?" she asks.

It looks like she's done hugging so I go back to my barstool. We don't talk for a minute. She's got green tea: she watches it steam. We hear footsteps upstairs: her mom? I turn my coffee cup round 180, then 360 degrees.

"It was you, wasn't it," she says.

"What."

"You sent me the pictures of Rich."

Saying what pictures would sound stupid so I keep quiet.

"Because one of my students. I didn't show him the pictures, I deleted them. But he did this computer thing with the message, and it told him the server was owned by a company called Astrakhan and he said do you know anyone that works there. It took him five minutes."

I want to say because it seemed right or honest, but she's talking.

"He said do you know anyone that works there."

She listens for a minute.

"I guess you thought you were doing me a favour? Rich wants me to come back, badly. He couldn't deny anything. But he wants me to come back."

Because it's gross, I want to say. You couldn't even talk about it.

"I know. It's better to know than not to know, something like this. Better to know. But I've got some big decisions to make now."

"I thought you should know," I say all dry-mouthed. Her lips are tight.

"I love him," she says, fearfully. "I love him. I can't believe I'm even saying this to you — do you understand me?"

"Don't be angry," I say.

Even though she's crying she keeps her voice down.

"What are you doing here," she says in tears. "What are you doing here?"

She looks at my face for its reaction.

"I didn't do anything," I say at last.

Her eyes flare up like she's going to hit me then they settle.

"You guys," she says. "You guys."

She looks away.

"You want to *pee* on women."

"I don't," I say.

"Why do you hate women?"

It just comes into my head: because you're soft.

"Isn't it better to know?" I say.

"We were trying for a baby, you asshole. I don't know what to do."

I sort of understand. But now she looks mean.

"I just thought," I start to say.

Outside in the car I think about when my parents used to fight.

IN SPAIN

She spent the first night in Barcelona in a blank hotel. The heat was moist, a shock. She was so tired that first night that she registered almost nothing, taking a packed orange bus from the airport into town, quiet as the industrial areas (this is what Spain looks like?) became suburbs, thinking that when people talked about Europe they meant something else. She left the next morning on a commuter train without seeing the city, following Jared's printed itinerary like a pilgrim.

When she arrived in the little town, Inez was waiting for her on the platform with a sign that said Aparthotel Ventis. She spoke little English, and Bella spoke no Spanish, let alone Catalan. Jared had spent the last five weeks mouthing vocabulary back to his iPod on the subway. But they tried with their hands and eyes and saying the same things again and again and smiling. At first Inez pointed to the train and didn't want to leave. She kept saying *Pensaba que iban a ser dos, dos*, raising two fingers. She was an anxious dark woman with kind eyes, and now she rubbed her neck: her big red wooden bracelet slipped down her forearm. Bella shook her head and lifted one finger and pointed at herself alone. Inez offered her a cigarette. Bella thought it might be the very first time Inez was doing this, as if she'd just been hired.

They drove along the cliffside road in Inez's little Seat. On the way she pointed out things that Bella didn't know the significance of: a denuded golden hillside; a cross in the bright scrub. Inez slowed down proudly when there was an especially bright view of the sea. Only when she pulled up at a house did Bella realize she should have looked more closely at the last village. There was a rusty bike leaning against the white wall. Inez pronounced "Bella" with rich, soft undulations, so that here she already had a different name from the one she was used to.

Looking worried again, Inez showed Bella the double bed and all the plates and then shrugged as if she'd gone to a lot of labour for nothing. There were coloured tags on each of the keys. It felt like no one lived there: but it was perfect. Just walking into the main room Bella was happy, the strangeness of the place, the glass table and then the balcony's red tiles. Seeing that changed Inez's mood. Opening the door of the hall closet she pulled out a child's bright Spider-Man umbrella, and Bella gestured for her to leave it, and they laughed. Bella hoped she'd come back. She imagined Inez making dinner, telling her family.

She hadn't packed properly, and the first order of business was a pair of sandals, then she'd be able to think. She was glad for her leather jacket. The cargo pants seemed stupid here. But of course she had her Dictaphone and pen and paper, and that was all she really needed. Best of all was the ancient stereo in the living room, surrounded on all sides by records. Unknown salsa groups and the moaning British bands she'd grown up to and German prog rock. She was going to listen to every one; she'd save them for nighttime. She didn't feel alone.

Jared was suffering. Friends came to see him, and he opened the door to them bleary, skinny and unshaven. There was nothing clean and nothing in the apartment, so he offered them tap water in cocktail glasses. He talked.

They'd started thinking about the future, he told friends. All their friends were couples. On the first night on holiday, he was going to ask her to move in with him. He had a ring for her, not an engagement ring. A present, a promise. What happened on Sunday, he told these couples, wasn't a fight, what they'd mostly talked about hadn't been this betrayal or that habit or that question of control or desire, but the vacation: the cancellation fees, the website of the car rental agency. She'd resisted making plans all along — now he knew why — and seeing her make this effort to be practical just hurt him more.

She didn't give him a reason, he told the couples. She wouldn't say a word about why: she said there was no reason. When she left, he found himself staring at the cup she'd drunk tea from: he resolved never to wash it. He told no one that. That night she called, and he found himself weeping into the phone, telling her he only wanted to love her, until he was saying it into the buzz that comes on after the dial tone dies.

She wasn't at her apartment, or if she was, she wasn't answering the door. He thought perhaps she was at her sister's.

He asked his friends to find out, but he knew they would not. He could tell they were satisfied, in a way. They'd found her odd and drifting. They'd liked her success, they'd liked seeing her in *NOW* and *eye*, but he could tell what they were thinking, that their two lives would have never come together into a joint project. You go from planning your life around someone, he said, you go from calling them from work twice every afternoon, to not knowing where the hell they are. I haven't even been to the gym this week, he said, not even one time.

Then he was laughing. It's not a breakup, he said, it's a car crash. Bam, she left me spinning. I don't know which way is up.

He lay on the couch nights, staring at the TV, wondering why. His parents would be happy, he thought. Friends began to call, too soon, trying to set him up with friends, friends working for big firms, new in the city, girls.

The strangest thing was not understanding what people were saying. Bella found herself staring at children, staring at workmen on street corners, trying to understand conversations as if it were something she could do with her eyes. Luckily the Spanish, ancient women dressed like ravens and bright-lipped men alike, were a people who stared too.

She woke up late each morning. She savoured the sleepy warmth of the kitchen and then took her coffee out onto the white patio and sat watching the sea, warming herself further. When she remembered dreams, she wrote them down in her green journal. She sat in no hurry, humming tunes from out of the night when she remembered them, wearing a scraggly T-shirt, wrapped in the pale blue sheet from the bed. Usually after coffee she went down to the dirty strewn beach to walk, sometimes she swam. A beigey-black mutt watched her for the first few days from one of the neighbouring houses, then started walking with her, jumping ahead to sniff at seaweed and plastic, then skipping back to her shins. After half a mile he'd disappear up a cement-tiled path, to visit a friend, she thought, and that was her cue to turn back, too. She didn't give him a name.

Afterwards she'd go back up to the house — no one was renting any of the other apartments yet, that was one reason Jared had wanted to come so early in the year, to avoid tourists. She tried to keep cheese and ham in the humming fridge, but even if she did have something to eat, she still liked to cycle down into the village before or after siesta to see faces. She recognized the flower lady, the boy with the red tricycle. People seemed unwilling to wave back to her, she wasn't a fixture yet. Sometimes she went to the internet café, sometimes she went to the pharmacy for supplies. She'd bought a phrasebook there, and she had it always and she never opened it. The druggists stood behind a window and a grille.

If it was later in the day, she might have a slice of tortilla at the Espanyol bar. The same two waiters worked every day in black bowties, shouting to each other to confirm orders under a tiny TV. A hog's head looked down at them unperturbed. She watched the old men of the village come and go friendly and suspicious, and though everyone eyed her, the waiters never talked to her except to take her order and give her a tiny receipt on an ashtray and then some Euros back as change. After, she'd cycle up the hill, unsteadily if she'd had a beer, sliding into the gravel next to the road, panting above the bushes.

She did think about what had happened, sometimes she was forcibly reminded, but one night down by the sea watching the lights on the boats setting out from the village for the night's fishing she was hugging herself warm and thinking that she was okay. That, like her brother said, you could leave your problems behind. All you had to do was get on a plane and six hours later they were gone.

I just got back from being taken out for drinks by Scott etc. I wonder if I'll send this even. Probably write it all out very carefully then hit delete like yesterday like the day before like the day before that. Yes it sounds lame but you don't care, so what do I care. Ha ha ha. There was an empty chair there all night of course — guess who. I kept thinking this next drink is the one that will make me feel better. Some drinks are built to make you feel better but I was ordering vodka soda, which I don't even like, in between beers, yes but you know why. I talked to this blonde chick at the bar, just pulled her away from her friends and started talking to her, she said she was an engineer but she usually told guys in bars that she was a secretary so they wouldn't be scared. But she told ME she was an engineer. I stroked her arm then in the washroom I called your cell, just to hear your voice on the message, it picked up right away. If you'd answered I'd just have said fuck you anyway. You like my angry voice, sometimes I think are you just doing this to provoke me? You took your ass away, that's the worst of it, mouth, that's the worst of it. I'm thinking what you want is some guy who'll slap you around, swear at you and make it hurt. Because you're in your own world, I was trying to bring you out of it but you're too damn selfish. You're always high. You're always in your headphones. Answer your fucking phone sometime.

She wrote songs. Every night she sat on the floor in the living room with the balcony door open so she could hear the night and watch the tiny bats flash past (then each morning the apartment was full of bugs again). She hummed melodies into the cassette player and wrote down the words that she was thinking. She played the melodies back and connected words to them, lines that she'd jotted down during the day, on the beach, in the café, or a phrase that had just hit her, that she'd got off her bike to sing. Those were the best lines, the ones that started intact — she could pursue them, build a theme around them, figure out which song they were coming from. It was like hunting, but it was also like collage, making something out of the strings and papers in her head. The one thing she missed was a joint to get her work started.

The last object she'd thrown into her bag was a little Casio piano keyboard wrapped in her one summer dress, blue daisies, because she couldn't face having to baggage check her guitar. Whatever you played on it sounded like elevator music, but somehow that was okay because playing plastic piano keys like this was something she hadn't done since she was thirteen. If she tried to play along with the records, it was like having an orchestra. Every night she'd sit down to say something until in the early hours she'd suddenly stand up, exhausted, her legs cramped, desperate to pee. One night she worked — she was really working, she knew — until the sky began to turn pink and white, and she walked out on to the balcony to see.

In the village a bar was opening. She saw the poster affixed to the green magazine kiosk. She didn't go the first night, but she went the second night. She sat by herself and watched the empty dance floor. She shook her head cold and vigorous when men came and pressed their thighs against the table, she didn't look up at them. There were old encrusted car parts hanging from the wall and six pictures behind the bar — the same picture six times black and white in six different coloured frames — a man from the 1940s with a triangle smile. The barman told her who it was quickly in Spanish, and when she didn't understand, he explained to her in good English: a tango singer who had died in a plane crash. His hero. "Your hero?" she asked. She smiled without meaning to. He was wearing a heavy pinstripe jacket and a tight black shirt with a slogan, one white sentence: Respect Authority.

Much later on he came and asked if she was a famous painter. The bar had emptied out when the kids decided to ride down to a nightclub in the next town on their little scooters. She was there almost alone, listening alertly to the syncopated guitar. His name was Ignacio, and he owned the bar with his brother. Opening a tango bar here was a risk, but they wanted to risk it: they'd owned an identical place in Argentina, and it had been a success, and then it had bankrupted them when the economy crashed, and they wanted to rebuild the same place here and repeat, except for the bankruptcy, *bancarrota*.

The economy's always crashing, that's what it's for, she thought. But she said, "This is a tango bar?" He put on a comedian's disbelieving face and laughed at her foolishness until she stopped him with her eye. "I'm not *from* here," she reminded him.

He was from Alicante, but he had lived in Buenos Aires for three years, his brother, too, he pointed back over his shoulder to the bottles. They'd both studied dentistry there. He said he wanted to stop talking and ask her things, he wanted her to talk, so she told him that she was a singer. He wanted her to perform that night, and she said no. He asked: "Tomorrow? What do you sing," he asked, "tangos?" She didn't feel like she was being played, maybe because he didn't have good looks or waxy black hair or stubble. He didn't look Spanish except for his skin. He was older, in his middle thirties or late, he had a giant shaved head and huge shoulders, and then tiny hands that almost seemed those of a palsied child or the little useless arms of a Tyrannosaurus, they waved around on their own program. He had great intensity, she could smell sweat when he moved. But there was also something effete: at one point he asked her delicately if she had ever worn couture, and she snorted her drink out through her nose. She told him she wrote her own songs.

He looked deep into his drink. And then cut her off to ask if she wanted another, flicking his own up to his mouth and down again. Then he apologized again for interrupting, said he really did want to hear all about what she did, *todo todo*, but that his brother was worried about business, and the anxiety infected him like a gas: there was a voice (his hand up by his ear opening and closing) saying he should be washing up glasses and doing the bar numbers. He laughed, he stood up, *Asi Luís no me castiga tanto*, he said. She didn't know what it meant but she liked a man who walked away from her. She said she'd wait, if he brought her another of these lime drinks; he bowed his head. She thought she might be able to buy pot from him. A white and grey cat strolled up the stairs into the bar and down towards the washrooms and winked.

Leaning her bike up against the wall, struggling for Inez's keys, she was remembering walking home drunk at two a.m., freezing cold, after playing two shows in a night, it was back before she really knew what she was doing, she was mostly waiting tables then. Feeling very poignant all of a sudden and liking it, she'd lingered to look in through the windows of a restaurant at the Indian busboy sweeping the tiles, as another cleaned off the counter with a blue rag. They were in their white shirtsleeves, and she had on that bright yellow parka that buried her. The chairs were up on the tables just like Paris, but then the boy suddenly swung the broom, a slapshot. She was on her way back to Jared's place, how could she remember now if he hadn't come to the show because he was working late that night or he had gone to bed early or because it was just too cold. She could believe anything now. All her memories were of nighttime.

After several nights she started to see a pattern. The songs fell into two categories. She could almost see it as two discs, as if that could ever be possible with her label. At least two of these album sides. Half of them were songs about straying, about other men. They were lusty and unapologetic and troubled, they made her look like a person who'd done certain things that she had not done. They needed to be arranged by someone loud and grim, she knew, but she could hear herself already: unwashed voice over the dirty male band. On the other side were quieter tracks, and she could imagine herself playing a second set, just these, with just her little Casio, risking the ridiculousness of it. They were personal and disguised, they were aiming at some sophisticated smoky ambience, and if they didn't reach it that was fine. These songs were about a warning she'd given him that he hadn't heeded. They were about being all fucked up to begin with and unsalvageable and a danger. She was a sea creature, she said in one of the songs: mermaids have bloody green teeth.

The songs were nothing to do with Spain. She was happy with how they were coming — for the first time in months she was happy with how they were coming. They weren't limited to him, but that was where they came from, you couldn't deny it. He wanted an explanation, so she'd give him two. The first side would tell him that she'd been looking elsewhere, and the second side would tell him he was better off without her. *Scissors and Stones.* If he chose the lie that was his mistake.

"*Hola? Es un mensaje para Bella.* This is a message for Bella. Who's possibly renting the apartment? Bella?"

Then his voice changed.

"This is a long shot. I don't know — if you are, please just call. People need to know you're okay. I've emailed and called your cell, and Laura has no idea where you are, and we're worried. It's not about trying to get you to call me, just call Laura, or Mark. It's just a safety thing, I promise. Just say you're okay. Okay."

She enjoyed the warm air as he padlocked the door, she listened to the hushed sea. Then they walked along the strand talking in English, and he tested her Spanish. He told her the wall they were walking on used to be the border of a Roman garden. He told her he was doubly a foreigner here for having been born in Alicante and for spending time abroad; no one trusted him. She told him he was way more Spanish than she was, and he said that wasn't difficult. "I blend in just fine," she said, and they both laughed. He spoke to her in French and was amazed that she didn't understand. He found it very hilarious that she was from Canada. When she asked why he didn't live in Barcelona, he said because of the sea. He rode her bicycle down the steps and fell into the sand and screamed out a song about canaries.

She followed him down grinning to herself and sat leaning back into his crab's embrace. At first she could barely make out the water. She asked him where the boats were, and he told her they were too far gone to be visible, their lights were around on the other side of the globe; but they were still there. His back was against the sea wall, and the sand was thin and cold around her feet. Still, she didn't like to dirty it, so she was using a flyer from his pocket as an ashtray. She told him about Jared in depth. About how he worked and how he pieced out the world. She asked him if he thought she was doing the wrong thing. He blew her hair away from his chin. First he made a joke out of it saying that many times the only way to deal with a romance was to emigrate. Then he was talking about how much he loved music, about how it let us escape — and she thought sure, maybe if you're the one *listening* — and he said she looked like Jane Russell. She swivelled and felt the wet on her knees and told him he must have been a boxer in a previous life or a cupboard and kissed him once, and his lips tasted like lemon peel and vermouth. They hugged for a while, but that was all. They became melancholy, and she said she had work to do, and he didn't try to hold her back. As she rode off up the hill, she imagined a man watching, shooting out a hand to try and force her back when she veered.

*

People milled in the green room, musicians and hangers on in long T-shirts, boys with uncertain beards. There was nowhere to change or do your hair — which was kind of the point — so everything happened here. Bella could hear one side of an argument about the playoffs though she was trying to listen to the band. A curtain hid an open doorway, and through that was the stage. Peeling flyers covered the walls alongside rubbed off torn posters. This room was the size of a kitchen, and ten people sat and stood and drank and some talked slightly more quietly at the quiet parts. At the back was a fire door pushed open into the alleyway down which ten thousand amps had been carried. The signs said you weren't supposed to smoke, and then one in black felt tip that she had always liked proclaiming that management took no responsibility for anything in this life or the next. She was sitting by herself, trying to create a little aura of calm, listening as the ReGifters reached the end of their set, listening for the response. She was used to playing bigger clubs now, but coming back here had its reasons. It was a preview show and a secret show and a welcome back.

She looked up and saw a dark girl in a shining dress, clutch purse. And Jared, wearing a suit and a silver tie. Bella stood. He looked stiff, and he wasn't supposed to be here until after, if at all. The message had to be sent first — what was he doing here?

She'd been back for a month writing and recording, rehearsing, and losing her tan until finally she was ready for tonight. She'd double checked he was on the email Picayune had sent, but she hadn't expected him to be there. Especially she hadn't expected to see him physically there. She'd thought she'd look for him from the stage and not make him out. She'd send the message, not care whether it was received or not. He was much more real than she remembered, but he looked light and victorious, it didn't fit.

The girl looked East Asian, or she looked Guyanese, her lips were brown berry. Her earrings shone, she was smiling, she was small and beautiful. Jared's hand guided her past beer bottles and mic stands and boxes of CDs and kids in dirty great boots. The ReGifters were filing back through the curtain all sullen. She could hear the PA wailing in their place and the heart pounding in her skin, in time.

"We're at the theatre," he said. "Down the street. And we have to go to the reception after. But we wanted to stop by."

"I'm Bella."

They shook hands, and Bella remembered strangers kissing on the cheek, in Spain. She remembered that black dog running ahead of her and back to her. For a moment she wanted to call it Inez, but she knew that was wrong.

She said it was cool that they'd come, and he said they couldn't stay, but Yana wanted to meet her, and they were just around the corner, so ... He looked down at her neck, and then at her body.

"I wish we could stay," said Yana, and Bella didn't hear her, so she said it again. Bella wondered what Jared had told her. With her black jewelled hair, she looked like Jared, too. She had a very fixed, attentive gaze.

"What are you performing?" Jared asked.

"Mostly new stuff."

"New?"

One night on the beach she had wondered whether it was a baby or a tumour she was nursing.

"I loved *Cycles*," said Yana. "It's really something to meet you."

Bella tried to say that it wasn't.

Jared watched, sculpted smile. Bella saw him start to check his phone, then stop. A gruff reddish kid in a woolly hat pushed past them carrying a case of empties, nodding his head at each step, and they had to move back and forth to let him through.

"You made me cry so many times, listening to that," Yana said.

Bella felt her head was too close in, she needed more space. And they were all being so polite and satisfied. The fury of it hit her.

"You're not supposed to be here," she started to say. She pushed past them. "You're supposed to be out there."

The ReGifters' bass player Ryan was telling her he was getting a beer before coming out to back her, asking how far in did she need him? and it was time for her to go on stage with her guitar.

DUMBO

Dressed in orange and dark red you walk down through the park to your bench, across from the glass-caged carousel, and then you stop, because a chick is sitting there, legs crossed, on your bench, at 5:08 a.m., and that's fucked up.

So you finger the beaded bracelet on your string belt, your rosary, because that's what you're supposed to do when you're a monk, and this little lady — she must be freezing, rice pudding face, under thirty maybe, dressed for a business meeting downtown like a TV lawyerette on one of your shows, like when you walked Chavo into his arraignment, he called it his arrangement — and she looks over and smiles. Oh, shit, *puto*. Remember to take your ring off.

Her eyes light up behind her big brown round glasses like a cartoon cat, and to get away you look over at the empty carousel. You put your hands together and bow a little. *Namaste*. Too bad she's not hotter, but she'll go away, she'll be on her phone, she's just being nice, she'll leave you to smoke, and not to think.

Little snow in the air, snow flecks gathering and parting under the shadow of your two great bridges. Where they touch, they disappear. Brown slicks in the scuzzy surface of the city river, that smell like paraffin, the light between you so grey.

But you can't just stand there. You sit. Feel her turn towards you, her whole body shivering, like she's been waiting. Like what in the actual fuck.

"Beautiful here. I love this place. I love the horses. You too, right?"

Nod, smile, like you don't understand. Dying for a smoke before you go over to your pitch, showing tourists pictures of a temple printed from Wikipedia in colour, hitting them up for donations. But how often do you get the chance to —

"Something there. There's something there, I mean — if we could all be laughing children. Didn't the Buddha say that? God, my brother would love you. He'd love your outfit."

She smells like the sea on an icy morning, that's a beautiful perfume, but when you cross and uncross your legs, under your skirts, you smell beef.

"I've been sitting here for an hour thinking about, you know what I'd really like? A *cigarillo*. Tastes like port wine. Bella always says I talk too much. But the world is beautiful, isn't it? People get married here! Look at the horses. They light up at night. It takes you back. These beautiful bridges. I could get married here."

She sighs.

"I walked across the Manhattan Bridge and I was going back in time across the generations. Fix your air conditioner! Get mugged for free. My uncle with a knife to his throat behind the Regal. I've read about Gairville. They told me stories when I first moved here. It used to be called Olympia. Oh boy. I don't know how long I can stay now."

She presses gloved fingers into her face and shivers. You watch as they sink into her skin. You keep your own face stony. Raúl picked you out of all his guys because you could make your face like a statue. At home they called you *el Chino*. You served on City Council, *la aldea*; you never lost a vote.

"I have to get on a plane at nine. Sydney Australia. Do you know why? It's an eighteen-hour flight. They do it non-stop now. For my sister. My little sister. Why sleep?

"She's twenty-five, she's a resident. A little doctor. It's hard for her. They work such crazy hours and for what? It's a kind of organized torture. And she said she'd had enough. She took time off. No one does that. But Bella does. I love that. But she's not on vacation. She booked herself a spot on this boat, to crew on this guy's yacht, from Bali to Sydney. It's some kind of race they do every year. A forty-foot yacht. In the Pacific. In the Pacific Ocean. She never even went paddleboarding up north, but you just ... you wouldn't know, with your vow of silence, your balls in your little purse. I think she was a genius. But that's not why we love her.

"She's so good. She's goodness personified. No, that's not true. But she tries to be. Selfless. Smile for everyone. And she said part of it was, at the hospital, it was the simple amount of suffering. The number of times each day you have to say No, just to survive, she told me. To get through the day. She's seen things now. She's seen things: four-year-old's heart drops onto the floor. No mother coming back for her triplets. Her fingers dipping through a red bag of eyeballs. Someone hid a rubber ducky in the cadaver's head! The stories she told. About those bodies."

You nod, you smile, you listen, and when she speaks again her voice is quieter, grainier.

"They were in a storm and suddenly beneath them a platform was rising. This creature ten times the size of their boat: the captain yells *humpback!*, red chains on its back, a hundred kinds of kelp from a hundred oceans. When it breathes it's like the sky roars, you can't feel your legs. And suddenly they're twenty feet in the air, yelling. And the boat, the boat shouldn't be in the air like this, and it's like it knows, they told me — suddenly it slams left, *snap* as the rudder breaks underneath, and the boom swings round a thousand miles an hour and Bella, that's my sister, she throws herself down to push the captain out of the way — she's a hero, my sister — only she goes head first into the head of the second mate, who was diving out of the way himself. The mate's fine but Bella's skull is fractured. Skull fracture in the southeastern Pacific Ocean. And she's the one with all the medical knowledge! They haven't seen land for eight days. A chopper came, eighteen hours later. That was three days ago. We just heard. Now she's in Sydney Australia. They don't think she's going to make it.

"The whale went away. Didn't even know they were there. Like a bug on your back.

"She told me once they have this thing that if you drown, you can be dead for twenty minutes and they can bring you back. Because it's cold. Your heart slows down to a halt, and your breath stops, but you're not dead. They can bring you back.

146

But she didn't drown. She hit her head. I wonder what was she thinking, while they waited? I wonder. Dreaming?

"She wanted to go on every rowboat in the park. Our tiny hands in our tiny red mitts. We used to sit on the what do you call it together, in the bows. Our dad would row us along. Our mom always made us stop. She always said it was time to go home. Why?

"I have to go. No one else can go. But I don't think I can go.

"There's no one else who can go. And Mark there on the shore throwing stones at us. There's no way he could go. He'd tell me to breathe different or eat more chickpeas. So I have to go.

"She made music. She played songs. She made barricades and threw rocks at cop cars all the way through school. Her songs are all I can hear.

"Maybe you can tell me something. Would you tell me something? Tell me what the Buddha would say. Because I saw her when she was born. I visited Mom in hospital. I touched her little skull. I mean her little soft head, the fontanelle."

Her hand is on your forearm, she is grabbing you tight, through the red fabric that came from your son's warm-up jacket, staring. You cut it off, and he cried, but you do what you have to do to survive. It'll help him, in the long run.

"It's Mark I'm worried for. Because I can do this if I have to. But what's Mark going to do? He can barely get through a day as it is. Because Mark and Bella, it was always the two of them, in our family."

And then she stops.

"Oh fucking Christ would you look at the time? I have to go."

147

She stands up, but before she can go, as she's digging around for her phone, she stops again, because you're standing up with her.

"Did you even understand a goddamn word I said?" she mutters.

You do your nod. You do your prayer. When you were a lawyer, back home, you took on cases like this: civil action. Duty of care. But that was a lifetime ago.

"Will you take this?" she says. "Take this and do some good with it. God knows the world needs it."

She presses two hundred-dollar bills into your hand. Then three more.

"No, take it," she says. "I don't need it. Say a prayer for me, for all of us. For my family. Sit shiva. Now and at the hour of our deaths. Read her the Book of the Dead. Or whatever it is you do."

The carousel lights up. It's never happened here, not at this time of day. Like a saint's fallen asleep against a switch. And in the air now, like baking smells, muted fairground music, like the music in a movie you dreamed of. Like the life you thought you'd have, once. And the growing frenzy of the animals, rising and falling bright against the grey buildings and the grey sky. Rising and falling. And the two of you in your skirts. And now she pushes her whole glove into her eye to wipe the tears away.

"Fuck," she says. "These are so stupid. I hate them!"

You're from the Dominican, and you live in a no-room apartment with a whole other family. You used to have a life; now you're fucking your sister-in-law; you don't know why. You'll get changed tonight in a Pret washroom because your son makes fun of your orange skirt. As if you're not doing this all for him. As if you didn't move to this goddamn goat-fucking country for him. For Chavito, too, of course. That's fair.

You and Chavito dropping tires into the water just because. When he didn't have to serve cocktails to women like this, and you weren't wearing a goddamn skirt and asking for money for a temple that doesn't exist like you don't speak Spanish or English or any language in this world.

That's why you come down to this bench, though it's not on your way. The crystal water. Thinking every morning here on this bench if you could only get some kind of goddamn break. You could start over. It would be sweet.

It is sweet.

You watch this woman go, you watch her ass slowly disappear, slender back curving over her phone the way we all do, and your face goes into that hard half-smirk your son brings out in you after two seconds of whining. You have five hundred bucks between thumb and forefinger. You're getting royally fucked up tonight.

LIKE
TRIUMPH

I was eating my dry Corn Flakes as Annie got ready for work. I think she said she loved me; she kissed the side of my head. Then she was calling out, Knock 'Em Dead. Then she was gone and I was alone with the baby. We didn't see each other much, at that time, me and Annie. There was her work, and when she got home from work she was all about Cassie and that made sense, and there was always the smell of kitty litter in the apartment. I heard myself say goodbye, but she was already gone. Already in my head I could see her at the bus stop, the wind fiddling in with her blondey-grey hair as she untangled her headphones. So I went to the sink to fill Cassie's fat neon sippy cup, and I saw a see-through plastic sheet on the kitchen door: Annie must have taken my suit to the cleaners for my interview, and I said Whoa, that's an expense, to Cassie. Then Cassie was saying *Ca*, this was her word for cup. Then she was screaming it.

This was a few months ago. I hadn't worked for a couple of years by this point and to be honest I was starting to wonder if I was really alive or not. Previously I'd done various kinds of communications projects, mostly around e-learning product breakthroughs, when my writing didn't work out, and I thought my experience was okay, but the only interviews I got were when the job description was a series of bullets written about me exactly, Mark Ferguson: gluten-free, Habs fan. Does not own a Vespa. Likes to have his neck pecked. Mildly obsessed with the travels of the Jesuits. But then something always went wrong in the interviews. I'd lose the use of my tongue and lips, for example, I mean I'd find myself physically unable to speak, as if some other version of me only not in a suit was standing there behind me, above me, spooning sand into my mouth. Or the opposite: I'd find myself talking about Self-Regulation, but too much, not able to stop talking about Self-Regulation, even as I found myself walking backwards like a black-clad modern dancer towards the elevators, smiling about Self-Regulation. I'd forget the basic tenets of my field — my own educational history, seemingly tailored to this moment, became a black hole to me. Or I'd just be thinking about Bella.

Annie said Don't worry. She said it was the economy, she said it was demographics. But the interviews slowed, and then the interviews stopped. That was my life I saw when I went running late at night: that train, stopped on the tracks, forgotten, lights on, emitting a high-pitched whirr through the windows.

We knew it was crazy to have Cassie, madness pure and simple. No one said it but we knew. Their eyes said it. The faith Annie had in me! At first it made me glow: Something's just around the corner! Then it scared me. It should have been her with Cassie, not me, and I walked around the apartment seeing dollar signs sprouting up out of Cassie's onesies, her multicoloured plastic kitchen furniture, her many tiny shoes that Annie always seemed to be exchanging with other mothers for slightly larger ones, her diapers, as if you could hang her on the door by them. She called for me, she clung to my shoulders, that warmth! But I wanted to be on my phone, alone with my thoughts. But I didn't want to be alone with my thoughts, because they were bad, at this time. It's not like in the movies where you put the baby down and read a book or screw your wife up against the banging bathroom door. When I had five minutes I thought about baking bread. I tried to improve myself, start running again. Meanwhile my brother-in-law Roger bought a boat.

When you look at yourself, when you look at your life, do you see a pattern? Do you see a thread? I pick up these moments, and I look at them now, but somehow I can't connect them, somehow I can't see them as relating to me. Like beads or marbles, there's no necklace. My moments are not my moments. They rest on the night table, by the call button that I press when I get the terrors and my nurses all ignore. Annie once said this way of thinking about things, it wouldn't help me any. But it bedevils me. It keeps me up at night. More than the beeping does, more than the whirrs. It's four in the morning and I'm thinking, Who am I? Who is this? Mark Ferguson.

Is this just a way of thinking, really? Is it just *habit?* At least it stops me dreaming.

We used to play pool on College Street: one ball would hit another.

At this time, I wasn't really sleeping. I never had that much sense of my own freedom, I suppose. The result was that I nearly died. I tried to kill myself; I got lucky. It could have been me lying shallow in the ground there, instead of telling you this. Six months in a hospital bed. Why'd they put a funeral home across the way from a hospital? Who does that? Do I need to apologize to you all? I'd need to get to know you first. Annie most of all. But yeah, it's probably too late.

Four-five months ago, so a coupla months before the interview, that is before I shot myself in the head and blew out a good quarter of my pre-frontal cortex, or so I am told, though it doesn't seem to have made much difference to anything, my brother-in-law, Roger, took me camping with his friends. They all brought rifles in these immense, ornate cases like for pool cues, like for special chef-brand knives. They were all expert. For some reason I wasn't expecting that, though I'd been told in the past that they liked to kill small animals in the woods. I guess I thought they were kidding about what camping was to them. But I wasn't understanding things as well as I used to. Not hearing instructions clearly. You know. That and my incipient deafness. My dizzy spells.

Hey, it's hard for me too, Roger admitted.

He was a huge guy, I'd say three times my height, my weight I mean, ex-police, now he's a bigshot defence lawyer but he drives a pickup truck. I pretended like I didn't know what he was talking about. A lot of the time, I just say nothing. I felt about an inch tall next to him, and I hated that. He'd learned a lot on the Force about Process, he said. What to do when things go wrong.

Everyone has a plan until they get punched in the mouth, we said together.

Jinx, he said. You owe me a Coke.

This loud and sudden crack came from the fire. These other guys were all asleep, visions of heavily armed hookers dancing through their heads. They'd ragged Roger about Erica until his puffy white neck got red. Your wife's so hot I have to wear sunglasses just to look at her. She rips the sky a new one. Your wife's so hot I —

I been there. You know that, said Roger. I've had times in my life. We all have.

Suddenly I wanted to be back in the city.

Roger flicked his can of Old Milwaukee off into the woods manfully. It went miles into the black. Even here by the crackling fire, the sky was so thick with stars that it looked like the sea. Or was it the other way around?

Roger checked his phone, muttered something about a stupendous restaurant he'd finally got Erica a table at. Vaping in the woods he looked like something out of that show about the highly sexed dragons that everyone was talking about the whole damn time, that I'd never seen.

Sometimes you're gonna want to pretend to be that guy, said Roger.

What guy? I asked him.

A man's glory is to ride roughshod into his enemy's lands, behead his enemy, enslave his enemy's sons, and make wash-shirts out of his enemy's wives and daughters, I thought.

Mark-o, he almost sang. You gotta let yourself be part of things. Take it easy on yourself. Why'd you always *push?* You feel me?

I was back in that moment when they let me hold a rifle. I could have pointed it anywhere. It was lighter than I expected. It felt like triumph.

I'd had a fucking ball that day, I don't mind telling you. They were good guys. Roger said it was nice to see me smiling.

Roger's tiny lupine eyes were orange now. Around them, his stubbly jowls were huge and demonic in the pumpkin-shaded chiaroscuro. I thought he was going to tell me something very personal, so I got in there first and said it was simple. We all have this voice in our head, I said. There's something wrong with mine. It's angry with me. I don't understand it any longer. It speaks to me in a language all its own.

I was lying, of course.

All you're doing is telling yourself stories buddy, Roger said, after a pause. It was as if he knew, as if I were transparent. As if he could read my mind. He scratched at himself in the sleeping bag. You might as well make them good.

Sometimes I'm so confident. I'd cut you all to ribbons. But sometimes I couldn't even look you in the eye.

Through a big huge yawn he asked me what I thought about this investment opportunity, the land for sale on the drive up we'd seen, his rifle range idea. I said nothing. Some days it's a victory to get my shoes on.

How's our girl? said Roger. I didn't know which he meant.

Good, I said. She just started on solids.

Then he was asleep.

I could have stayed out there forever, just the lickety flames and me. I could have walked into the forest and never come back.

He'd said he had an in at Callway. Guy on his hockey team. We'll look after you, he'd said. Nothing bad ever really happens, was what he said. I know a guy, he said. We're gonna make you whole again.

It seems to me possible that when people talk about heaven and hell and call them superstitions they're missing something obvious, which is the temporal dimension. It seems to me eminently possible, likely in fact, that our great era, with our ability to see via location tracking where in the grocery store our personal fucking grocery shopper Rahul is standing, is basically Marx's hell. But that in turn the Dark Ages was the cold wet Hades of the Greeks; the solitary life of the salaryman is the hell of your social cave-dweller. This life I'm living now, with my toddler and my recycling: to my nineteen-year-old poet bike-riding snooty self, it would be hell.

Shortly after or before Roger's hunting trip I said to Annie these last two years have been just fucking horrible just entirely horrible just hell I've been falling down a mountain in burning hell for two years and I'm alone and I'm burning up. These interviews, I said. I don't sleep.

She said nothing for a while.

Then she said, Not entirely horrible. I knew she was talking about Cassie.

The size of her eyes. Like saucers. My wife and my child! What was I doing to these people? I didn't want Cassie to end up like me.

This needs to stop, I thought. I didn't want to end up like my dad, reeling out my own madness. Who was I kidding? I missed Bella. I missed talking to her. She was the only one who really read my stuff, too, and I always listened to what she said, because it was like she got me, and now she's gone. My sister on the boat. My sister in the water. Whereas Laura doesn't give a shit about us. She never did. She was always on her own track.

Do you think there's part of you that wants to make it worse, Annie said. Do you think that's something you could try to change maybe? Sweetie?

I resolved to, that day, and it helped, for a while. I stopped drinking, I prayed, I started on the little pink pills, triangular. I did some woodworking, I did Tai Chi, I learned to cook, I meditated, I stopped complaining, I stayed in the moment, I read. If we'd had a piano I'd have learned to play it. I stayed off the porn.

It helped, for a while, but, you know, it was still me doing it.

What did I do next? On the day of my interview. What the fuck even happened? I put on a show for Cassie On Demand. Callway hadn't called to cancel, that was something. Out of the smeary window it was contractors in white cargo vans, a hearse with its long tail of black town cars and little purple Funeral signs stuck into the hoods like birthday candles. Jogging moms pushing strollers tutting at the mail carrier's truck parked halfway up on the sidewalk. You're going to hurt some little kid! It's the law! I guess to the rest of the world the day your life nearly ends is just another day. I saw the hypnotherapist cruising ever so gently up the street the wrong way in her cream-coloured Merc, and the moustachioed local painter who provided home painting solutions we couldn't afford. The day's recycling bins stood gaping like baby dinosaurs in the nest. It was high summer but already golden leaves were falling, spiralling, all their little loves dying; and still the sun failed fully to pierce the branches of the chestnut tree, as, delicately, a red-tailed hawk spread his white underwings wide to come into landing on the rusty skewed spire of our church steeple. Twitching, he glanced over his great territory once more, and prepared to hunt again.

See? I fucking told you. Poetry.

An episode of Backyardigans lasts twenty-four minutes and eighteen seconds, from character reintroduction to final handholdy goat song. I showered with the door open, under the broken light fixture, going over my Strengths (they'd said the interview would have various steps: after the usual sit-down, a practical element with a verbal-oral component). Then the bathroom went white, like the space behind my head, and when I came to I was in the fetal position, the water spraying my back. I almost killed myself sliding out of there, that would have been funny, and of course I wasn't dressed or shaved yet and I called out coming sweetheart! She was still inert though, in her own world. And it was okay, I didn't want to see my big head, older than it was supposed to be, my red eyes, anyway, so maybe it was better not to shave. I'm not going to show them I care. Annie had instituted a one-show limit for brain development, but I had to find a fucking tie so I put on another show, thinking I'll be able to do more for her brain development if I can afford to buy her some books, okay? I grew up in a house full of books. But the TV was always on in the corner, that was my mom, the corner of the kitchen, in front of the fine china, and I turned out okay. Cassie has the softest hair in the world, the sweetest smell. I'm going to do better, I promised.

Her mouth was moving funny. Or I'd had a stroke. No, I was fine. Out of the side of her mouth, Cassie said, Describe a client conflict you recently resolved. Where do you see yourself in five years? she asked me. What makes you laugh? Do you believe in luck?

Kind of, I said. I guess. I thought about it. Well, bad luck maybe.

Can you make me a list of your triumphs and disasters?

Sure just let me —

Make me a list of your triumphs and disasters.

I looked for them around the apartment. I needed a car to drive through the city to find them, but without a job I couldn't afford a car. There's really no way out. I was by the door, trying to kick the stroller open, still in my boxers. I really had to remember the wipes this time. Cassie was gnawing on her own fat arm, basting it in a layer of spit. Oh kid, I said. Then my phone rang and I didn't recognize the number. Congratulations! said a girl who sounded about twenty and kind of into me. You have been selected to win a free Taiwanese cruise! Stay on the line for more details. So I did.

I got a feeling, Annie said, before she left.

Stop twitching, Roger said, in the forest hide. It's not a dance party.

I didn't love anyone that much. People are a lot of work. My life at this time, it was all cortisol, all shoulders.

This is the problem. With Cassie it was a long walk from the bus stop. Their house was brighter, the lawn was perfect. A black balcony stuck out like a surveillance post. Orange trim brought the windows out garishly, Erica's latest improvement. Sometimes a set of plates would suddenly appear in our apartment after she visited, a lime-green chest of drawers for the baby would be delivered as if by magic, fully assembled. Suddenly I felt exhausted.

Hey Ric, I said.

Hey Gorgeous, Erica said to Cassie, Hey Nibs! And then, Tyler's in the playroom with Milinda. I'll take her. Let me take her. And then, over her shoulder, You want something? Coffee is on.

Milinda's voice soared along to us from some cavernous reach of the house and then closer and closer, like a siren. How did she move so fast? Could she float? I wondered silently if she had help; she might need divine intervention, with Tyler. She was standing in the doorway now, impassive, red-panted, red-lipsticked, the Queen of the Nannies. Once I walked into this hallway and she was doing CPR on one of Tyler's stuffies, a pink dinosaur, and he was doing it alongside her on another (a Labrador pup). They looked deranged, and it was not a little disturbing. I was not a little disturbed.

Coffee is on? That didn't sound like English somehow, that phrase.

We laughed at Cassie laugh at Milinda. She had instantly forgotten my existence.

Erica was speaking. What's with your coat? It screams don't hire me. I'm wearing a beige trench coat from the seventies. Meet me in a parking lot for tips on Watergate but whatever you do, don't hire me, I *billow*. Seriously, Mark, take one of Roger's jackets. I got him some new finery at Harry Rosen's for his birthday, and he's never going to wear it, he won't know. Take it! It's upstairs. It's big around the shoulders, it's fine, it's better than that goddamn blanket you're wearing to push your grocery cart along. Jesus Christ Mark do you want this job? Now tell me sit down are you all set? Are you focused? Are you centered. Sit, you can get it later, just tell me what you're feeling now. Sit. Her voice was like caramel.

It's an index perhaps of the confusion I was feeling at this time in my life that I sat, meekly, with Erica, whose roots were starting to show in a way that made her look even more like our impression of her at Roger's stag party, a few years before all this, I think, when everyone dressed up like her, and Roger's best buddy Astor duct-taped metal mixing bowls across the front of his fluorescent lemon gown and we did karaoke. Fuck, that was a night to forget, too.

At her kitchen island, the two of us at this silver island in a vast expanse of kitchen ocean, just across from each other, with all her Mexican suns on the wall watching me, some of them smiling, some of them scowling, like the masks of ancient dead comics and tragedians, her hand on my forearm now, her bracelets jingling, this is Annie's older sister, they love each other, they talk in the evenings. She'd just come from her trainer. She knew way more than I wanted her to about my day, my plan, and she didn't let me get a word in, she was all yoga pants and glossy orange lycra and exuding good things, good energy, the sweat she's sweated out, the sweat that still dappled her lovely shoulders, I guess they used to call it vibes or chakras and your place in the energy circle and she was kidding around with me, too, she was super earnest and then she was kidding around with me (what is it with people and their ability to *speak?* I barely say anything, anymore. I keep my counsel), she was making cute faces, saying this coffee maker cost us a thousand dollars, and I don't know how the goddamn thing works! and talking to it like it was voice activated, and yet somehow I knew how human she was, how desperate, underneath it all, like all of us, how much fear she felt, like all of us, but then fuck, I watched her turn away from me like we were in a nightclub like when once in a while, two hundred million years ago, a girl would turn away from me only then to grind against me thinking maybe I had pills for her because of my reticulated way of dancing, it's not that long ago we used to go dancing, the four of us, and she reached up to grab two tiny espresso cups, the ones with the goat and a fawn on them they'd bought in Italy and I was like, fuck. I just wanted to grab her, all your laws and customs be damned. An incredibly rich smell was filling the room. It's grinding, Erica said to me, and winked, and I wiped the fucking idiot grin off my face or I tried to. Could she read my thoughts? Was I actually made of glass? Somehow I had the craziest sense of déjà vu.

For some reason I really hoped Annie hadn't told her what my little pink pills did to my ability to hold it in for more than thirty seconds. It helped in its way because Annie was too tired most evenings for that kind of thing anyway. For some reason I remembered this one time, we were here, in this kitchen, I'd come in from the vast den where Roger and I were watching the Colts fuck the Ravens up the ass for the eighth time that season, it was as if the NFL was organized as some kind of monstrous zoological sex crime, Roger said, Only in football shirts, I'd said, like an idiot. Tripping up those three little steps I thought of the stuffies one on top of the other. I came in to grab four more beer and Annie was here with Erica, Annie was in this seat, Annie had her head in her hands, she was staring down dead eyed at her beautiful reflection in the marble countertop of the island, and when I came in Erica folded her arms. These Mexican suns on every inch of wall space, staring down at me.

They talked. I know they talked.

For some reason I thought they were talking about what happened to Bella. But Annie talked to me about Erica too. She was born with a scalpel, Annie told me. She's an emotional vampire. She sucks in pain, but she can't let herself feel it.

No, you know what it is, Annie says, correcting herself. She wants to help. Annie always sees the good in people. It's her selflessness.

Now, these days I mean, my hospital days, let me tell you, Annie brings Cassie to see me, sometimes, but more often it's Milinda who does that. You know, Milinda, she comes to see me every day. Tyler and Cassie do thumb wars as we talk about what Jesus might want from us. Doesn't he *know?* I ask her. Why doesn't he tell us? She leans forward and clasps her heavily bejewelled knuckles together on the side of my bed and we pray, she leads us in prayer.

Every night I dream I'm a monk.

Every night I dream I'm a monster.

My Dear Great God, she says, Above us all.

The sparrows come and go, but she's here every day. She tells me about Tuay Bareg, where she's from. You're funny, she says. She winks at me.

She's good people. There's goodness there. You could say it's a fire hose, sure. But you could also say she's taken me in hand.

I was thinking about you in India, Erica said.

How *is* Roger these days? I asked and made some questiony shooting sounds. What's the big fella up to?

Fuck Roger, she joked. I told you, India. I want to try something with you. Close your eyes. What do you see?

Her face now. Young, like an Annie who doesn't have to work.

Nothing.

Think of India. What do you see.

Shit in the streets, I said. Dead babies everywhere.

Jesus Christ Mark I knew you wouldn't take this seriously.

And then, Oh I wanted to ask you. We're going to Bermuda for Christmas. Can you take Tyler? She bangs the counter with the bracelets on her lower forearm like the suburban Wonder

Woman she is. I don't give a rat's ass, she says. I need to do something for *me*. Milinda's going back to the Philippines. First it was her mother was sick, now it's her father, if you can believe it. But we need the time. You know. Us. Sugar? she said, touching my forearm again. Her nails are white. Her fingers are tanned.

Four, I confessed.

She spooned them out.

I worried for Cassie for a second. Tyler was a beefy, threatening kid. His mouth looked like a sewer grate. And like we were in perfect synchrony Erica went to check on Milinda and so I started going over my prep again, and when she came back she asked me, What is that? Can you even read that?

Sometimes, I said.

It was my list of triumphs and disasters.

She looked genuinely concerned and about fifty years older.

I guess from her perspective the charts and crossings out might seem sophomoric, I mean horoscopic, but I explained that I was just going over my plan for the day.

So what's that she asked, pointing.

Wheel hubs, I said.

What?

The wheel hubs on Cassie's stroller are rusty. I need to fix them, but I don't know how.

What the fuck is a wheel hub Mark?

I forget things. Things I need to do. Squeaky taps. The light fixture in the bathroom.

For some reason even though I couldn't think of the thousand other things on my list, I felt close to tears.

Hey, she said seriously. Hey. It's okay. You got your resume together. You sent it in.

That was Roger, I said.

You're trying, she said.

Trying —

Not everyone tries, Mark. Some people lie on the couch all day like it's all they can do. That's a real thing. With Bella, that's affected all of us. That changes things. But you're going to look back on this time, I know it. Breathe now, breathe in, breathe with me.

I was kind of glad I'd told her actually. It gave me a sense of release. We breathed together.

You have a daughter who loves you, she said. And a wife. These are good things. So what exactly is the problem?

Maybe it's just a matter of timing, I said, calmer. I mean, Why don't I get to go to Bermuda? It's hot there, right?

The grass is always greener, Erica told me sagely. She paused and then she went on. We don't talk, she said. He's training for an Ironman now. They lift trees, he says. That's where he is all weekend. Training. Why are we going to Bermuda? So I can see him. Because I don't see anyone. Tyler's a monster. Milinda looks down on me. There's a lot of scorn there, you know? A lot of resentment; she was a nurse in her country. It's just me here. Look at us, she said. Look at what life does to you. We were trying for a second. Another Tyler! But I've got past the point of thinking the answer to everything is in him, you know? His body. I'm well past the point. My friends, they all know.

I already knew all this from Annie.

So is it cool if I borrow that jacket? I said. After a long moment she replied with, Go on up. Rockin' the stubble, she went on, without looking at me.

You're not hardcore unless you live hardcore, I sang back to her as I left the room.

Shoes off please, she told me.

They had an upstairs because they had a house. Annie said she didn't want *things* like them, but I wondered. You're funny, Erica said, that was in my head as I went up those three little steps to the landing. I heard my daughter yelp, and almost lost my footing. Perhaps it was Tyler; one child is much like another. How does one person thrive and another fall into the murk? Tyler was already a brown belt. But we're all people, aren't we?

Now the carpet up here was light blue and made of hand-woven hamster hair imported from Persia, flown in by unicorns ridden by eunuchs and naturally phosphate free. It washed your socks as you walked upon it. My toes sank and then I floated up a foot above the ground, I bounced. Walking on the Moon, like The Police.

I got the jacket, a beautiful emerald oilskin waterproof thing, from the closet and purely out of innocent curiosity I moseyed over to their bedroom to see where it all happened. Their playroom. There was a machine in there, I don't know what to call it, with eerie little red buffing wheels, and this bathroom the size of Brazil and no doubt cuffs and ropes in the closet here, chokers and gags hidden behind Roger's many suits. There was an island in the closet, too. And the small red box about the size of a toaster, just where Roger had shown me, a couple of years ago, when it was just something to talk about, on the top shelf. He kept a neon-wrapped key on his keychain, and the other was taped to the top of the inside of Erica's bedside table drawer. In case of intruders, Roger said. Bad guys. He pointed at the side of his nose, his moustache. You have something like this for Annie, right? Sure, I said. I mean you've got to now, the way the world is, right?

The handle was black and the muzzle was silver tinged with blue, as if cut from Antarctic diamond. It was smaller than I remembered, like when you go back to your childhood room. And heavy in my hands, heavier than I expected, like triumph. The yellow chamois rag it was wrapped in was oily but at the same time so incredibly soft. I wiped my hand off on one of his linen jackets. He knew how to fix a light fixture if it busted; he'd be fine. In a different portion of this lunchbox there was a cardboard box containing two cartridges.

Oh, a lot of getting ready today, I said.

I didn't want to be harmless anymore. I wanted to be harmful. I put the box away and the weapon in the jacket pocket and breathed in the cedar deeply and then came back into the bedroom. I left the green jacket on the bed so as to take a final pre-interview watery dump in the dream palace.

I was wiping my hands on my beautiful dress pants and What are you doing? Erica said.

I smiled to see her. I might ask you the same question came into my head. Dry mouthed, I said, I'm trying to relax.

She just stood there, so I unbuttoned the leftwards inner button at my waist and pulled down my flies for her politely.

I was wearing clean boxers for the interview. I'd put on some of Roger's cologne.

Er, said Erica. What —

Here, I told her, with a little indicatory gesture, and I waited.

What the fuck are you doing Mark, said Erica gravely.

You want to . . . ? I said, indicating. You're here to . . . ?

Her eyes were like plates.

It'll just take a minute, I added. Less.

What do you think is happening here? she said very carefully, hand nearly at her side, a little splayed out, holding her phone.

You can make me whole, I told her gently.

She burst out laughing, like she couldn't hold it in anymore.

The room was shifting. It seemed I was stepping backwards towards the ensuite.

Oh well, I thought. Okay.

Oh sweetheart, she said, and I stopped. Oh, I'm sorry. You're just not cut out for this, are you?

For what? I asked.

Was now the right moment to do up my pants?

She was laughing. One hand over her eyes.

This life, she said, still laughing, still grinning, with great sadness. People.

Oh well, I thought. Okay.

You're a funny guy, she said. She came closer, but she didn't put her hand on my cheek, thank God. She pushed me back playfully. I felt her diamond ring digging into me hard, through my lapel.

These moments.

Hey, don't worry: when I left I took his jacket with me. But I didn't say goodbye to Cassie. My stomach was hurting.

On the bus I felt like I was forgetting something. It was her.

These moments.

So I went to the interview.

Nailed it.

They loved Mark Ferguson, whoever the fuck that is.

There's that old J.Lo video where she's leaving the city, dumping jewelry, briefcase, walking down to the beach, pulling her clothes off, gradually removing from herself all the things on her that are not her, singing away the whole time like a schoolgirl. Now she's like some sexy grandmother. Only for some reason it keeps going through my head. What happened next was kind of like that, only people were calling me the whole time. Annie, Roger, Erica, even Callway. Why was no one texting me now? When Annie called for the fourth time I answered.

How's our girl? she said. How'd you leave her? Are you done yet?

I told her it was delayed, they were running over, and I asked if she'd put my shoes somewhere weird and she said by the door silly and then her voice inflected by concern asked me what I was wearing. You're not wearing your clown shoes are you, sweetie? I didn't tell her I was wearing Roger's beautiful green hunting vest.

We need this Mark, she said. We really need this. Then, Roger's calling me, she said. Oh, Erica's calling me. I better check Cassie's okay. Go get 'em, Tiger! she said. I can pick up Cassie after, she said. You left the stroller, right?

Okay, I said, to no one.

We used to laugh, she said one night. Long ago. You used to tickle my sides! I said. You told me I looked like a violin, she said. We used to laugh, long ago.

I tried to buy a bottle of lime-flavoured Gatorade but my card was rejected.

Accept love, said Milinda, in her church. A choir of her, singing it out. All the nannies in red gowns. We didn't have a nanny; I was our nanny.

Standing still, on the street now, I saw people with jobs. Men in light grey suits speeding to the elevator banks. Women in light grey skirts laughing with one another. Indistinct chatter, the subtitles would say. They went to the gym after a big win. They made out at the bar. When they saw something that they liked, they bought it. They were on a path. None of them had little backpacks, I noticed, so I took mine off and left it by a curvaceous low cement wall.

I didn't want to be walking anymore, and soon I found that I was running. When Roger called again I threw my phone into some handy bushes. I took my shirt off and left it on the ground behind me and I ran. It was hard in these shoes. I'd put the jacket back on though, and the gun thunked up and down with each step like I was carrying a stegosaurus in there, I was sure it was going to go off and shoot me in the ass, but it didn't, it didn't, not yet anyway. But I ran.

I don't know if I told you, when I was eighteen I was offered a track scholarship in the States. I had the fourth-best under-eighteen time in Southern Ontario for the 1,500 m. That was me! It's actually not that long ago. But I said no; I stayed with Annie. On and off. She was always there, in the background, my lodestar. Though sure, I broke up with Sonia a few times along the way too. But it's always been a way for me to be myself. It's always felt like that anyway. I had my running friends and my work friends and my Annie friends, back in the day. I ran.

Cassie was born. Again she came late into the world — two weeks! What was she doing all that time in the womb? What was she waiting for? A better option? I was at school again, I was crying. I wrote some stories too. How did the animals do it, I wondered. I mean live. You never saw an insomniac dog, an insomniac fish. I could see my sisters. I could see my sister. I could see my dad. I checked my pockets for my list but I'd discarded it somewhere. The sky above me looked strange now, like Erica's face. Boy you fucked up big time now, said the cloudy sun out of the side of its mouth. I should at least have tried to kiss her. Perhaps she would have tried to kiss me back?

My T-shirt was drenched through. I sat on a bench to grab my breath. In the downtown park, near an artificial lake, there was a green hut down on the nearer bank, and next to it a floating bright blue dock led out on to the water where ten or twenty midget orange rowboats were waiting, bobbing, tied to floating plastic planets. I'd brought Cassie here to see them, but the City had a wildcat strike, and the boats were all taped off, and she cried. I was happy then.

A dangerous-looking elderly couple in matching tracksuits was eyeing me so I leaned forward and looked between my knees. Everyone else in the world was at work. A train flashed away silently, and then another, like duelling swordfish. To the left was the lake and to the right an old train platform, the old industrial tracks that had been taken over by commuter rail. They were building a hotel across the way. It was Cassie's naptime. I hoped Tyler hadn't bitten her again.

The thing in the sky, it was like a yellow ring around a heart of black, and at the same time as it was on top of the sun it was also opening up a hole within it, beneath it: under the blue of the sky, all is black, after all. Our bright blue sky is kind of an illusion: when there's an eclipse, in the middle of the day, you see stars. The terror of this, the beauty. And how thin a veil it is, that keeps your life together, that makes it make sense — that obscures the truth of it? — and after all, it's just a story.

Peek-a-boo, I said.

They were freaking me out a little with their staring and their gestures, this antique version of me and Annie in love on our honeymoon outside Paris, Ontario, so I went away, I went further. I had to get into cover. There was an old wooden outbuilding on the other side of the fence. I poked through and made my way over to the train tracks that I loved. The metal-plastic caught on the jacket, tore a line, but who gave a rat's ass really, not me. There was a big box store, two of them, over, across, but not here. Here I could sit, in between, on the tracks, amidst the drinks cartons and the serried leaves, my knees wide open now. I was still thinking about Cassie's wheel hubs. If I fell back, if I hit my head. Sure there was a sound in the air, but that was beautiful too. And when I think of what I could have been! And what I was. The books I've loved, how little help they were to me at this moment. And yet now they seem more real to me than my own life. But had I even read them? My movies, my shows, had I even watched them? I mean, did I *attend?* These marbles, these threads, they are mine and they are all I have. And they don't seem good or bad now, they just seem like what they are. Somehow they've been given to me, and I had to, if not look after them, at least study them, or preserve them, or react to them. It is my task to honour them. And to let them be, because if they aren't good then they aren't bad. My pile of stones. My hill of beans.

Be it ever so humble, Annie said to me, when we came back from her birthday dinner at Roger and Erica's place. My God, she deserved better. When they redid the sidewalk outside our building we wrote our initials in the concrete, she leaned down onto one careful loving knee holding Cassie for our daughter to leave a handprint. What the fuck is wrong with me?

She says they weren't calling because they were angry; they were calling because they were concerned.

You're the donkey making your choice, like the philosophers say.

After all this, once I'm better, we're going to have to move to Guelph. It's the only way.

But sitting on the tracks by the park, I shot myself in the temple.

Milinda says that's where you aim, if you want to live.

She is right.

177

HUCKET'S
TECHNIC

At their first interview, Robideaux seemed to Procurator Lamark still to be carrying too much of the jungle with him, too much of the barrens, for it to be quite safe for him to return to his wild places. The first thing this sojourner needed, Lamark thought with his nose, was a good bath, and then possibly a good supper.

According to the letters that the Intendant Poignard, Lamark's superior in the Order, had sent before him, Robideaux had lived for several years in a Siamese monastery, where he had learned the language of the Talapoins and their ways. He had served in Brazil and in the Comoros. If he plucked a hair from his garment, who could say whose it was or whence it came? He was returning now from the mission to Quebec; his name had become known after the martyrdom of his brothers at the hands of the painted Iroquois when he alone was spared. On his return to France he had been invited into the young Queen of Savoy's carriage, it was said.

She wanted to know, the gossips said with a smile, all the customs of all the worlds that Robideaux had seen. The boys in College hall talked of his coming and nothing else.

To Procurator Lamark, who was still a young man himself, less than a year into his role, Robideaux's appearance, in every sense, presented the threat of disorder. He was generally surprised still at the Intendant Poignard's absence from the College, at the distance old Brother Jacquard, who should have been his aide and a font of knowledge, kept from him, at how little help he had, as if he was expected to know how to do his work by instinct alone, from his first day. But his superior Poignard told Lamark to assess, and Lamark intended to.

Robideaux's huge open face brought to mind Dürer's Self-Portrait Aged Twenty-Eight, with the lustrous hair, the uneven, querying gaze, its patterns of dark and light, and the giant hand. Only Robideaux's beard was thick and matted, and he bent his face down to Lamark's Habsburg teacup, with its thick golden rim and heraldic shield of winged demons, like a man who had not had a drop of water to drink in many days. The gracious bird-bone porcelain shook horribly in his hands; his mutilated sausage fingers could preserve nothing delicate. Lamark liked precious things, while Robideaux had been everywhere that was savage. Had it helped him in his soul? He is quite literally not all here, Lamark thought, with another of his little smiles. When Robideaux laid off sipping and was staring at him again with his great, endlessly open, endlessly searching soft eyes, Lamark suggested that he could work in the gardens, when he was ready. You can push a wheelbarrow, I am sure, Lamark said.

He looked down at Poignard's letter again. Fingernail sized pieces of crimson wax lay at his feet. Poignard instructed Lamark to assess Robideaux's suitability, after all he had experienced, for any pastoral work whatsoever. His very soul might have been imperilled, Poignard wrote with a flourish (or more probably, of course, it was his secretary, or one of them, who had such wondrous calligraphy and turns of phrase). If found unsuitable he could go on to the Hospital at Bouges to recover fully; it was safe for him to live there. He ought not to return to the world, Poignard was sure of that (no matter how much Robideaux might desire it). His ideas about the ways of men were already untoward. Speak to him three times and then report, Poignard instructed; your voice will have weight in this.

And so my College is made into the second circle, Lamark reflected, where souls are weighed; and I am Minos, with his tail, and I must judge.

Lamark was aware, as he read and reread, of Robideaux's vast eyes sweeping across the room, taking in no doubt the symmetrical stacks of paper arranged in two rows of three, the flint and tinder on the desk, the dried wildflowers from the north meadow, the tattered edition of Petrarch from the Library Lamark had set himself to repair months ago, and had not yet had time even to examine properly. Then Robideaux was observing his own hand, close to his face: a minuscule black carpet beetle (a worthy part of God's creation too) crossing his curved fingerthumb caught his attention entirely.

Sometimes one of the fathers took a class to the village zoo to see the Incan llama, the bear cubs, the darkened yak, the toy unicorn, and of course Leonardo and Olivier, the two old snow

183

tigers they had named in Poignard's honour and to mock him. The zoo was the king's gift, not unrelated to the presence of the College in the outskirts of La Flèche, of course. The Father made this trip out of zoological interest, perhaps; or perhaps he needed to fill an empty afternoon after examinations. Once, in his first weeks as Procurator, Lamark had gone along, too, and come eye to eye with the wordless sad beasts that he was now reminded of by Robideaux. What had this man seen, and how had it marked him? It was curious to note that they were the same age exactly, to the day, the Procurator realized: they had the same birthday. The same horoscope.

Robideaux was suddenly rising to leave. He was patting down his robes at his thighs. He apologized with great ostentation for his frayed raiment. Then, at the door, he stopped, as a townsman will stop at the end of an informal conversation, not a confession, to reveal the true reason for his visit, as if it were the hand on the door that enabled him to speak freely. But Robideaux simply said, looking all the time at his feet, that he hoped to have a long and productive stay at the College. Then his eyes rose, and with shining face he asked, in his curious, frank, open manner: Lawrence Hucket is close by, is he not?

Hucket occupied an unusual place, within and outside the College walls. A transplanted Irishman with perfect French and as many moles on his nose as there are on the grandfather in that famous painting of Ghirlandaio's, he was living in the village of La Flèche as he worked on his great book. By virtue of some unwritten arrangement with Lamark's predecessor that neither Lamark's man Emile nor any of the Brothers (even

Jacquard, the music director, who had been there longer than the gargoyles) could quite explain to Lamark, Hucket used the Library, walked in the Cloisters, and even dined, most evenings, at the long dark tables with the Fathers and their boys, regaling them with tales of his wild youth, joshing them (Lamark hoped) into a more secure faith. Hucket could screech at table like a red-tailed hawk; he could whistle like the wind among the reeds; he could make his voice into each of the barmaids' at Le Sanglier in turn and offer invitations best left unrepeated. The Procurator had to bite his lip, literally, at times. Hucket was a man of the world, it was true, but beneath his japes there was, Lamark thought, or hoped, a deep broad soul. Above all, his was a nature that lived to question nature. Lamark liked the boys to see him, to be in the presence of an accomplished man. But he tried to keep a watchful eye nonetheless.

As the scholars' bell rang, always at the same moment, like the black tulip closing, Hucket would excuse himself and depart, humming the College song as he went, ducking his immense secular head under Lamark's archways. Hucket worked late into the night in his rooms above Le Sanglier, a silhouette at a table, a hand unspooling, Lamark was told. He got reports from the town grocers and carriage-men. Hucket's stove was full of balled up, crushed papers, they told him; his sheets littered the halls. He entertained village women and had broken two chairs and made holes in the walls where he stored what he called his archive. Then one night this past month, Lamark was told, Hucket burned all his papers. The work was botched, he wept drunkenly in Le Sanglier, to anyone who would listen. He had wasted his life.

But one morning, passing by Lamark in the Cloisters, Hucket said, It is coming, it is coming, with a frown. I almost see dawn, he said in his old, confident, always slightly hoarse voice, though Lamark had not asked him a question. He was writing about pockets, he said, about things transported. He was a strange man, Lamark thought. Truth be told, even after these many months, Lamark felt he did not know how to talk to Lawrence Hucket.

It is Hucket whom scholars come to ask about, these days, when they visit the College. One has come today. Learned men in wigs, they place their ornate japanned snuff boxes on the Procurator's shining lacquered oval side-table with a clink and ask, as if fevered, about the origins of the *Technic*. They open calfskin notebooks, smile with brown teeth, and ask what subjects were discussed at the College tables on particular evenings decades ago, tied to moments when, they believe, Hucket came to some logical pronouncement or other to put into his book; but as far as the Procurator remembers, the talk was mostly of the venison, the anise. More abstract subjects included the breeches worn by Italians in the south of that land, the various types of wood one can use to make a viol, he tells them.

Hucket worked alone, in his rooms in the village; he kept his book to himself. His genius — a secular one, let us remember — was a thing he kept apart. Men of learning come, but also men of parts on their grand tours. The College is becoming a stopping-off place. The innkeeper's son at Le Sanglier calls himself a hotelier now and expounds on metaphysic!

These scholarly aristocratic visitors, jowled and powdered, ask if the Procurator kept any of Hucket's possessions from this time: his Nuremberg pencil, perhaps? His kettle, his stove, or his long coat? His hat. (For these were examples he'd used in his writing). As if Hucket were a saint. As if, after Hucket died of pleurisy a few years on, the Procurator had gone to Le Sanglier to sniff out relics. As if Hucket's great and horrible atheistic text were the product in some way of his time with the Order. They savour that irony; there is nothing men of ideas love more than the whiff of scandal. Lamark has read in the *Technic*, more than once, over the years, but to him, it is all equations. It takes him back to a time he prefers to forget, a time when much was still unsure.

When snow falls in the College, as happens rarely, except around the time of the Founder's Feast, it seems to Procurator Lamark that the Cloisters are transformed into a shimmering, half-hallowed hall. What is inside is brought out. A dream architecture. And yet it is strange to see this place become strange, because he knows every flagstone. Some of them he put down himself, with Tams Argent, the village builder, breathing over his shoulder. The new stone scraping the light hair off his knuckles; his blood breaking through the skin without pooling, or gathering into anything more than its lattice. You want to rinse that off in the pond, Argent warned him one time he tripped and fell. That fucker'll go right green.

These days the Procurator begins his devotions late at night, once the worldly business of the College is complete. He does it to calm his will, but he finds it more of a challenge now than ever before. Thoughts buzz at him like the rain against the windows. He wonders what prayer is for; he wonders who prays. One has to have immense control, he reflects. He does not sleep well, and it is not unusual for him to rise early and walk through his Cloisters in the half-light. Off he goes to walk in the footsteps of his Hucket and Robideaux, but he goes alone, accompanied only by himself, reflecting, king of his little world.

Hucket would borrow a boat every Sunday — every Sunday! — Lamark remembers, to study the warblers on the seashore. They were birds from far away, from North America. Their tiny bodies crossed the seas for three days, flying alone. Here they alighted.

Hucket said as he left the hall thirty-four years ago, on the night the beast came and made of himself the new College emblem, with his breath very redolent of port, that there was no need to take this world as a vale of sorrows. *Sursum Corda!* he dared to quote. Lift up your hearts!

Lamark's body feels brittle now. He wonders what happened to his sense of humour. At this time the College is silent. Halfway down the complaining stairs he touches the bust of the Founder, a King he has met in person, on the nose, half respectfully. The bronze has brightened there, on the tip, weathered away by many young fingers.

One has to have immense compassion, the Procurator thinks, as his sandals brush through the lush, light, powdered snow, walking again, always walking. I must learn to pray again, he thinks. I am free from sorrow when I am at prayer. Why do anything else? Why do I occupy myself with *tasks*, he asks himself. But he finds himself walking. Who is it who prays, he wonders. Who is it who walks? Did he wonder about such things, before he met Hucket and Robideaux?

As with every year, there are preparations to be made for the Feast. The little animals, the College's secret tenants, the voles and rabbits, leave their little tracks in the snow, as do the village women who come to Mass before the secular day begins. Breathing heavily, Brother Jedwab passes on his way to bring out the morning's bread in his huge round woven baskets, to stand them up on the cart. The day is beginning. There will be the rehearsals with the choristers, his meetings with individual Brothers, his argument with the cook. Another Hucket scholar wishes to see him this afternoon. Are there enough of the two-footed candles?

Do other people not stop, Lamark wonders. Do other people not recall?

The light this morning, with the sky sharing the grey-blue of the sea, seems to the Procurator to be the perfect physical instance of the grace of God. I met a man, and he dazzled me, he says suddenly, staring out at the waters, speaking out loud, as if he might say this to his visitor this afternoon. I was so sure of him! For a moment.

No one, he suddenly realizes, has ever come to ask about Robideaux.

*

Lamark was punctilious, you will know by now, and he would never have said that anything was "fast" approaching. He knew that the future always approached at the same, untroubled, terrifyingly impersonal rate. And yet the Founder's Feast was

189

hard upon, and it made him fretful: Poignard would be there. Upon taking up his role the Procurator Lamark had occupied himself consciously and conscientiously with the worldly concerns of the College, not at the expense of the boys' or the Fathers' souls, of course, but certainly as a value worthy of consideration. His predecessor had been neglectful, Poignard had told him. When it rained, the crypts flooded. The building might be new, but it was immense, and like a ship of war, it had to be maintained constantly. We won't save many souls, Lamark told Tams Argent, a man of means and status, if we spend all our time bailing out water.

You're right, old Argent said, and rubbed his cheek, and spat. Our Lord didn't send you to build a fucking ark. Je m'excuse, he added, tugging at his flat felt hat. He was always moving, always touching at something.

No, it was Poignard that sent me, Lamark thought.

It was true though that this storm was extraordinary. They wore their long coats, and the ducks had absconded. Tams' brutish son Tams Junior was with them, and Lamark was surprised at how freely Argent swore in front of the boy. He was no longer surprised that Argent didn't watch his tongue in *his* presence. His other boy, Robert (known universally as Little Argent), was in his first year at the College. This elder son, Argent said, would take over the business; he didn't need book schooling for that. But he wanted young Robert to sing for royalty.

Last night Little Argent had been there when, as part of the celebrations for the forthcoming end of term, the boys had thrown their new captain of monitors into the pond to thus mark his ascension. His hat with the goose feathers lay wrecked and waterlogged at the pond's edge: long goose feathers, good for a blanket, not the ducks' squat little things. Little Argent had roared with exquisite delight.

You'll need new gutters there, said Argent, pointing a long finger upwards with unexpected grace, where the water was flushing out. Lamark was amazed at the gesture for a moment. Somehow old Argent was for all the world one of Bernini's shepherd boys.

There it's like a fucking waterfall, Argent said. And that's coming down over the windows to the crypt. So that's your answer: gutters.

Who was this man? Lamark wondered.

Gutters! Argent said again, louder, gesturing, as if he were speaking to the idiot in the village, Sonie Levesque's gargantuan, perpetually whistling, wheezing boy. He repeated himself, features sharpened by avarice.

And who's going to pay for that? Lamark muttered.

He could speak more softly now, as he preferred. The worst of the rain had passed. With Argent he always found himself putting on a worldly voice and a worldly face.

I'm just a dog that shits where it wants, Argent said, shrugging. Je m'excuse.

Let us concentrate on the tower roof, Lamark said. Sufficient to the day.

Very well, Argent replied. But who put in that piece of shit? he asked, stomping away in unlaced brown boots, their mouths wide open around his ankles. The Procurator could fill in the rest from experience: They knew nothing! Lamark hummed to himself. They had cheated the Brothers, he continued. Of the College! But of course the Brothers were always too trusting, Lamark sang. They didn't know how the world worked.

They used copper! Argent spat, speaking first to his boy and then to Lamark, without changing his tone. Copper for a gambrel! Would you believe it? Who did it?

According to my papers it was you, Lamark said, silently. You and your father before you.

Argent kicked at the paving stones, personally aggrieved, the way Lamark felt when he found a book out of place, or when he saw a boy's cravat, loose and woggle-less. Such men ought to be strung up, Argent was swearing. Don't you ever, he told his son knowingly. Anyway, I'll have to send away for it. It'll be months.

It exhausted Lamark to have to be so cunning every day. The tower was where Robideaux slept, a floor down from the top. They had just come from there. Robideaux, you will not be surprised to know, seemed to own nothing, not even a book. He did not complain about the trickles of rainwater passing down the stonework and rough plaster. Perhaps he drank from them. He had nothing that could be ruined. And he spoke to every man alike, Lamark had noticed, be he the Pope or the goat boy. It was a quality that Lamark, cut from so different a cloth, admired vastly, in spite of himself.

And in fact Robideaux and Hucket were passing by now, as was their wont, easing through the cloisters like a swan and a duckling, or were they a tortoise and a hare, unmindful of the soft spray of the rain off the wide balustrade, each with one arm around the other's waist, the way they walked at the University in Dublin, where Hucket had studied and lived, before coming to La Flèche under a cloud, after some college prank gone wrong.

Nice weather for the ducks, Hucket said amiably to the Procurator as they passed. Are you keeping your eyes on your final reward? he added, indicating the tower, but he spoke on before Lamark could offer any rejoinder. We too are discussing monkish modes, he continued, walking on, speaking half over his shoulder now. I mean other than your own.

Lamark scurried up to walk alongside them.

My Plato and my Aristotle, he said. Strolling in my groves.

Robideaux seemed peeved, like a hunter forced to hold back his bow by a gust.

Oh, let's not go too far, Hucket replied. His strabismus added to his detached, unworldly quality, as did the long black cloak he was always seen in. Sometimes he lost his balance; sometimes he stopped; but never after a glass of port, Lamark had noted. He wondered sometimes how much forethought there was in Hucket's stumbles.

Robideaux had freed himself and paced forward, and now he stopped and turned back to face them, his huge soft eyes wide open, shining brightly, lighting up, as it were, his delicate, thinly cut, hungry features. He might look like a jewel glinting its yes and no from a courtier's neck, but he walked always in a soft cloud of his own making.

For example the Talapoin monks, he said in a fervent tone. They have no sense of mine and thine. But they are no fools. They study disquisition and debate, they know all Cicero's tricks. Only they have come to them by their own roads.

You call them tricks, Hucket mused, but his face showed cautious interest. He kept his back to the rain.

Their immortal souls! Procurator Lamark said, looking upwards, and crossed himself. Robideaux did not follow suit.

I have told you about Nagasena and Milinda? Robideaux enquired of Hucket.

Remind me, Hucket replied.

Are these heathens you met on your travels? the Procurator said, to include himself. Plato and Aristotle, he added humbly.

Robideaux had not spent a single day in the gardens, he realized. Nor had he made any splash with the boys, whom he ignored as if he did not even notice them. He passed all his time with Hucket, talking. And he had done nothing with his awful beard.

They speak in the *Milinda Panha*. This is an essential text, or no, albeit, an important text in the Talapoin philosophy. In which the sage Nagasena denies that he exists.

Lamark laughed. So who denies it?

But Hucket was waiting, and Robideaux continued as if Lamark had not uttered a word: The queen Milinda says she has a chariot, Nagasena recounts. But what does she have, he asks, if she looks closely?

His hands gestured, made the shapes. Here are wheels. Here are reins. There is a horse, standing off to one side, one supposes. Here is a foot stand. Where is the chariot?

Well, it is all these things together, Lamark began, but Hucket was speaking over him.

If one looks at the parts, then where is the whole? Hucket asked himself, with legal precision.

Or what blindness to the parts does one need to think that there is any whole at all? Robideaux said.

So that, seen wholly, there *is* no whole, Hucket finished.

No chariot, Robideaux said.

Nagasena has thoughts, said Hucket thoughtfully. Nagasena has feelings, one feels.

He pronounced these unusual foreign names, Lamark noticed, just as Robideaux did, without any difficulty.

Hucket went on: Or let us say, rather, there *are* thoughts. There *are* feelings. There is joy, there is reluctance. It comes, it goes.

Where is Nagasena, midst these accidents? Robideaux asked.

Where is Nagasena, Hucket repeated, wonderingly.

This is to the purpose, Robideaux said. And then as if thinking of something new, he went on: Nagasena is a body.

But Nagasena's hair falls out, said Hucket.

His teeth grow yellow, said Robideaux with a smile.

Over time he grows —

Over time he changes —

In Greece of old, said Hucket, turning to Lamark suddenly, each plank in Theseus's boat the Athenians preserved in dry dock for his glory is replaced as it rots. Tell me Lamark, after a generation, is it the same boat?

What? Lamark asked.

Now they both looked at him. Hucket from his great craggy aquiline height, with sharp talons dug into the cliff, Robideaux all eyes, like a furtive thief poking his head out of the fakir's woven basket.

Where is Nagasena, asked Hucket, quietly. There was some awe in his voice.

Queen Milinda looks around her state room, said Robideaux. Her heart beats faster. She approaches one of her huge mirrors. She touches at this vision of her face. For the first time, she wonders.

Do they have mirrors? Lamark asked. Large ones?

Their palaces are places of extraordinary beauty, Robideaux replied in a careless tone. Far beyond ours.

This moment, said Hucket. That one. His eyes were closed now, his back to where it had been raining. Each moment but a passing moment, he said. Each moment so convinced that it is the lasting whole.

When there is nothing but the parts, Robideaux said. Nothing but this moment, that one. Do you see?

What? Lamark asked.

This was the rhythm of their speech. It was the rhythm of conjoined thought. To Lamark it was as if one person were thinking and speaking, not two. He could not be sure, afterwards, who had made which statement. Two voices humming to one another in the dark, adjoining, correcting, harmonious. A duet. He observed from the outside in some pain. He wanted desperately to speak, but had nothing sensible to add.

Yes, exactly, said Robideaux, his eyes shining darkly, like the meteorite discovered in the quarries, on Lamark's desk, late at night, in the candlelight, when he couldn't sleep, and returned to his papers, this rock that, Brother Legg assured him, quietly, was old already when Christ was born and walked the earth ... And how could that be?

This is what they believe, Robideaux was saying with urgency. You understand.

Never had Lamark felt more strongly that he was with one man who was walking out of the desert and another who was a djinn with keeping of a reservoir of cool water. It troubled him. He feared what such discoveries could do to a man, such questions.

They had come to the end of the arcade and had to turn left through the gate that led to the deer woods or turn back. Only now his attention was taken up, out of the corner of his eye, with the spectacle of Argent, against the fountain, beating his elder son about the brains. He would have to speak to him, again. He set a terrible example. The boy was whimpering now, his eyes full of hate. But only a year or two now, and he would push his father back.

You do not consider me foolish, said Robideaux, in a voice that throbbed and pulsed. You do not consider it idolatry. As ever he kept his hands behind his back, Lamark noticed, hiding his knotted, wasted fingers.

I consider it a false and injurious religion, Hucket replied after a weighted pause. Suddenly the sun lit their faces.

Yes, quite, quite, Lamark added. One might as well ask the College goats when they expect our Lord to return. He spat, the way Argent did, into a brown puddle; the stain stayed on the surface, the colours spread and separated, the whole iridescent spectrum forming an arc, God's bounty.

They have no sense of mine and thine, Robideaux said again, as if in a dream.

It seems to me they have no sense of *mine*, Hucket averred.

Unless of course they are joking, he added, mirthful.

Yes precisely, Robideaux said, following his own track. Do you see — that perhaps we are misled? All our woe, he went on feverishly. That comes and goes. What if this is all accident, he said, suddenly louder, spinning around. We think it is whole. We think *this* is whole. Even as we know it is not.

I do understand, said Lawrence Hucket, in a voice as calm as Robideaux's was afflicted.

Violin and cello, Lamark thought. Jacob and Esau. Port with old cheese.

If this Robideaux is but an illusion! Robideaux said, patting his own chest. What a release! It would mean we can be freed from constantly remaking this … we do not need this, this … Pain need not last. Walls come down, they tumble like old Jericho's, he was shouting now. One can live instead of hiding. His voice suddenly changed, doubted. I wonder if you do see, he said, looking at them both. But then found itself again: It is nothing! It is nothing! It was a jig he was dancing in a circle.

A puzzle would be resolved, Hucket said, calm. Or rather, the pieces are swept off the table entirely, and one can play at a different game. Let me add, your coming here is a gift. Your thoughts complete my own. There is much I have been contemplating: what you say is serendipitous. For it would be abhorrently, ridiculously, and uniquely limiting, would it not, to think oneself one and the same, trapped in a case of bone, when even the case and bone has changed and grown and replaced itself, atom by atom, over time.

And this was how he would phrase it in his *Technic*. And this was what the scholars would quote, in later years.

But for now Robideaux stopped Hucket from speaking further, grasped his arms, held on to his thick sleeves. The two men gazed at each other amazed. Dazzled, one might say.

It was a cold day, Procurator Lamark would remember, but many times Robideaux wiped the sweat from his forehead.

He had had fevers, he had told the Procurator at their first interview, on his voyage back from New France. Terrible fevers. He had been close to death and not known himself. The Iroquois monster that eats men's souls had come for him; but he had seen the Lord's angel standing by his bunk in his rolling cabin; they had spoken elbow to elbow, like this, he had told Lamark. His bloody vomit sluiced along the floors. Did the angel care, or did he judge? The wendigo slobbered, but the angel stayed until it finally bested the savage beast, like and unlike Jacob. At last Robideaux had been told that it was not yet his time. Then his fever broke. Lamark had listened, affected, feeling that his heart was passing out of his chest, was become a dish to be shared.

Now they walked on without him. Now the boys were coming from Arithmetic and Rhetoric, filling the cloister with exuberant chaos, with only the ones from the very youngest years silencing themselves when they saw him. That inconstant blond last-minuter Bruyère gave Lamark one of his wise-beyond-his-years looks.

And what of the immortal soul, that remains? the Procurator asked that night, as he washed his neck with rough thin cloth.

What about the soul gathered in the eyes of the Lord? You use the word 'I'! Is that not proof enough of what we all know already?

These thoughts came as if of themselves. He had been thinking of a possible change to make to the College grace. But his complaints came of themselves.

And God sees you, he said aloud, kneeling in his cell. God sees you in your boat, and his love guarantees that it remains one and whole! You may not see God, you may avert your eyes with all your will, but God sees you.

You want to live, moment to moment, but God sees the monster within you, he added, in a different voice, the beast you hide. What of the beast, Hucket?

This was Lamark's second interview with Robideaux. He feared that he would have to report the man's excessive emotionality, the nature of his attachment to strange ideas, to Poignard, when Poignard came for the feast. He feared the consequences for Robideaux and for himself. And he had no idea what he could say about Hucket. Keep one eye on your philosopher, too, Poignard had said. It was to this time that Lamark dated his first insomnias.

*

Because it is possible to lose oneself entirely in events, Lamark realized suddenly, stopping in a cobbled lane in the village at three in the afternoon, not far from the watchmaker's, on a day of such glorious wintry brightness that he had to shade his eyes in order to see. It is possible for a whole day to pass in action, without devotion or contemplation, he thought. I have spent this day arguing about ostrich meat, about the correct colour for a rosette, about the difficulty of finding straw to stuff the effigy of the Founder with its oddly bright skewed mouth (Brother Jacquard was terribly intent on the effigy being perfectly prepared, as — Lamark struggled to follow the details — there was a College tradition of it having to fight off a beast from the deer woods as the last step in his installation as Procurator) — only, no doubt, for Poignard to stop at a Chateau on the road, tempted, no doubt, by one of his decadent orgies, to send a messenger boy in his place, and all this effort would be in vain.

And so who are you on this day, Lamark asked himself in Robideaux's pressing baritone. A man can fritter away his entire life, he answered in Hucket's sombre bass. If this whole day passes, who has seen me? Was I seen? Oh Plato, oh Aristotle, Lamark grunted aloud, with your questions. He had been through the training; he was no fool. He fingered the crucifix on the chain around his neck and said a prayer. Here in a lane off the village square, near the cobblers' bridge, he heard the College bell ringing, from so far away. The pitch of the note resonated along his ribs now, but was the timbre sweet enough for Poignard? You can spend your whole life thinking about *things*, his voice began again, and never see the thing itself.

As a boy he had been very surprised to learn that Jesuits had to shave like other men. And then as a novice how surprised he was to learn that his mentors had spiritual conflicts!

He had thought that they were perfect in their faith. It was Poignard who had educated him in this, in fact. He had asked Lamark to consider what had drawn him to the Order. If a man were perfect in his faith, why would he trouble himself to act in the service of the Lord? A certain trouble is a requirement, Poignard had said to him, rubbing a lazy nail along his silk eyebrow. But not too much trouble.

Procurator Lamark was haunted by his visitors, these birds of passage. They threatened his work. The very topography of his being was tilted; all thought and emotion moved in their direction now, down certain narrow corridors that he disliked.

And now I am reflecting on myself reflecting on my reflections, Lamark said, aloud, to nobody. He had not been himself for weeks, he suddenly felt.

So yes, it's not the *whole* day that has passed in events, he reflected.

He walked on.

I must act.

Tend to your work, he insisted to himself. Keep soul and body together here in one place, at one time, he told himself. One step after the other. Repair the roofs. You, too, have been assigned. You, too, are assessed. In the squares of this lattice, there is infinite space to act.

But wait: truly, do you act on these matters, or do these matters act on you?

A villager with sunken cheeks whom he didn't recognize passed him, tugged at his cap, a visitor perhaps. Lamark revealed nothing. He was, anyone would say, the picture of control. A cartwheel cracked, and twelve ripe turnips tumbled out of a basket down into the muddy tracks, and there was an accepting cry.

He had slept fitfully again the night before. Waking up before dawn, he had considered rising from his bed. But then upon falling asleep again, he had dreamed of Hucket and Robideaux. They were together in a fur-skinned tent around a leaping fire, laughing, joyous, dancing. Then they sat, and they passed a long pipe around, one to the other. They offered it to him.

Dawn's dreams were prophetic, the ancients said, but Lamark was not so sure.

Had he dreamed of escape the night before the feast, he wondered later, or of some new confinement?

But even as the cornets sounded, Argent, incredibly, was patching a wood panel the colour of Amazonian chocolate. He gave the lantern affixed there a loving pat that made the light wobble eerily, then scurried away with his little footstool, like a beetle with its dung ball, his shadow growing and stretching. He winked at Lamark, his face made grotesque.

Je m'excuse, thought the Procurator, as all stood to attention around him in the semi-military manner to which he was still not accustomed. His older colleagues, these men who railed and truckled and groused behind his back at every decision he made; the boys who drew cartoons of him, giving him immense organs of generation, on the stable walls. Should he pursue this, should he investigate? His man Emile had asked.

Patrice L'Amoreux, the youngest boy in the College, spoke the grace from under his red curls in nervous but flawless

Latin. Then the servers, boys from the village, came out bearing sea bisque. Their white-gloved fingers poked out from under the salvers like their smirks. Lamark noticed that the Habsburg cup from his study was here at his table-setting, oddly. He could use it for the toast. Perhaps it would bring him luck.

Lamark was not hungry in the least. He turned to say something he hoped would sound urbane. In his head, he went over the speech he had to give in praise of the Founder, after Jacquard's wrestling match with the animals that he was still confused about, but even as he began, his hurried thoughts were scattering to other places, their favoured places, as if his mind were a harras of broodmares over which he had no control.

He regretted how much had gone wrong already this evening. Into the mustard yellow senior salle before dinner, Hucket inevitably floated, patting each suit of armour on its plackart. How did he do it? Making his usual paradox about the College wine being far too good to drink, and then acceding to the steward's proffer, chuckling away with Brother Jacquard like conspirators, two men drawing visible breath together in an alley. The choir had been supposed to sing them in to their supper as they ascended the stairs, but they had scattered somewhere, unforgivably. Lamark would have to speak to the director, Jacquard, who was also charged with theatrics, where had they gone to? But still, the immediate earthly result was each turning boy carrying a candle up the turning stairs in silence, the only sound the sound of their steps, each face focused, and the effect was ethereal.

But where was Poignard? Even with the spoon in his bright orange soup, the Procurator had to have one eye on something else. Well, a thousand souls were in his charge, while Hucket's nib scratched across his manuscript. It matters, Lamark thought, how we are seen. He wished it did not.

A little ways down the table someone, no doubt meaning well, asked Robideaux to tell of his travels. It was the Wendat, as Robideaux insisted on calling the Hurons of Ontario, who had rescued him, he began, speaking the way he always did, as if taking up a tale half-told, his hands hidden in his lap. The Iroquois had drawn their hideous designs on his skin, on his forearms, on his chest, he said, as if to make him their own possession. Robideaux did not show them now, but Lamark had seen the ribboned creatures graven there on the slender back, on the iron forearms like stovepipes, when he'd come in on Robideaux bathing. They had kept him tied up on what he called their village green for many weeks. Their children, their boys and girls alike, younger than the boys of the College, liked to cut his flesh away for a pastime. They placed hot coals on his closed eyes for their sport. On their festival days they set him free of the tree against which he was tied. But he could not run; he had no spirit left. And where would he run to? There was nowhere to go. No Christian within five hundred miles of me, he said. And I was in the world, Robideaux said, and in this world human skin crackles like fat pork. He spoke coldly and in detail, and no one ate, except for Hucket. The boys in their hubbub, with one monitor at the end of each table with his shining brooch, knew nothing, but how they would have loved the tale.

They treated me like the doll in your quad, Robideaux said to Lamark offhand, speaking of the effigy of the Founder with horrible familiarity. He had a gift for unbearable comparisons. He was speaking very quietly though, now, with no energy, and Lamark wondered what new disaster had befallen him.

At times I felt myself to be looking down on myself, said Robideaux. I did not feel myself to be myself. I watched things happen to myself from above, a little ways above. There is my body, there is my flesh. And now a young boy with tightly braided hair approaches Robideaux once more, bearing a knife with a brown bone handle. It happens, I have read, in moments of extremity.

There was silence.

Their immortal souls, Lamark said quietly, for he knew something was expected of him here.

Do they have souls? someone asked.

Do *we*? asked Hucket, without looking up.

Listening to music, Brother Paul commented, one may be transported. The boys in the choir have celestial voices. Such a pity they were not directed to accompany us in tonight. So much falls away, under new administration.

Ecstasy is the Greek term for standing outside oneself in this way, Hucket noted.

In drunkenness? Brother Legg, the logician, asked with a laugh. In dreams?

The boys in the choir, Brother Paul repeated. Most individually themselves when most adjoined in service.

Lamark intervened: Let us rather understand *ecstasy* as an opening up to God within.

But in dreams, Robideaux picked up, Are we most ourselves, or most strange?

These are puzzling questions, Lamark said, hoping to move on. He was in a fur-lined tent with these men again; sweat broke out on his forehead.

Among the Iroquois, Robideaux began, ignoring the general shuffling of feet, the global irritation that Lamark noticed, wondering at the change of mood. It was as if they had all decided they had had enough of Robideaux and his adventures, or perhaps it was that Robideaux seemed to be speaking only to Hucket again, in a conversation with its own rules. Even Brother Paul pushed his plate away, glumly. But he supported his skull on one hand so as to hear better.

Among the *speakers* of Iroquois, I should say, it is considered important to literally realize one's dreams.

I have begun the arrangements to dry out your rooms, Robideaux, you'll be glad to know, Lamark said.

Dreams may be messengers from above, said Brother Paul to Robideaux.

Dreams are toys, Hucket said, in a definitive tone. We owe them no responsibility.

Argent says it will only cost us half the Founder's bequest, Lamark began.

Am I here? he thought. Do I command?

You teach a child to care for his toys, don't you? You teach the boys here to watch over their sandals and skirts, Robideaux was saying with feeling. The speakers of Iroquois will travel for days to recover some object seen in a dream, he went on. A trophy, a kettle, or even a dog they have dreamed of acquiring.

He paused with meaning and then looked up and down the table, and then he said with his usual curious tone of naïve delight: In the winter, a feast may be organized to realize the dreams of some important man or woman.

You compare — ! began Brother Paul.

I learned much from them, said Robideaux in his most fervid way. It is common, he went on, among the speakers of Iroquois, to request a dreamed-of item from some other person. It is unheard of to deny it. Whole societies, nations, organized by dream economy! And then as if discovering some new connection: For they have no mine or thine, Lawrence. Like the Talapoins.

He seemed angry now. His eyes were burning. He was speaking only about himself, Lamark realized. Hucket said nothing, for once.

Is it possible? Robideaux said. That the whole world is wrong, and only we, here in France, are right? With our mine and thine. And if there is no mine?

No one answered. Perhaps no one understood.

Do you dream, Lawrence? On one's deathbed, he went on, at the hour of one's death, it is said, one may dream a whole life one did not live. Experience it fully, breath by breath. It is as if the veil is torn.

There was silence.

Robideaux slumped back into himself now, like a man shamed by his drunken harlot of a wife in front of his church and family. He looked like a drowning man thrown a thick round loaf of stale bread. He was for all the world one of Bruegel's abandoned peasants.

This was Robideaux's catastrophe, Lamark reflected: he might speak Iroquois and Siamese, but the truth was that he spoke only one language, his own.

I never dream, said Hucket, lightly, as if commenting on the spices in the soup. I attribute this to my inability to make mental pictures. But if you want the cast-iron kettle from my rooms above Le Sanglier you are welcome! I have no need for it.

I will come for it tonight, Robideaux roared, with a strange delight, joining in the general laughter.

I will tell you how I came upon it, Hucket began, and launched into another of his ludicrous, scatological stories.

I dream about you, Robideaux said later, slumped into himself now, having partaken of much wine and not caring who heard. My other life.

And the Procurator saw that when Hucket went out to refill his pipe and convey his warm compliments to the cooks in the kitchens, with his usual sardonic parting cry of *Sursum Corda!* lift up your hearts! Robideaux watched him walk down through the hall, every step of the way, as if his eyes could go nowhere else.

Lamark's man, Emile, leaned close into his ear with warm male breath, like the black bull's steaming breath in the blue pastures. Poignard had sent a messenger boy with letters, Emile said. Poignard himself would follow tomorrow. But my speech, Lamark thought, first of all … but he swallowed as if unaffected, he nodded, he sent Emile away and then with a loud snap of his fingers summoned him back.

Be sure to give him a warm bed, he said, and a good enough dinner.

As a ramekin of raspberry mousse was passed down over Lamark's shoulder by a sweet-smelling but sullen village boy there was a crash at the end of the hall. One of the long tables had suddenly collapsed with a bang. The scholars from Saint Jean's house in the corner were laughing, loud and high-pitched. Lamark's anger did not immediately dissipate when he realized that they were screaming. A knot of them fled suddenly and squeezed themselves up against the wall, while others shouted. Plates clattered on plates and saucers cracked on to the floor, and the wine sloshed off the tables as candlesticks shook and fell. Pure terror and ball sports, Lamark thought, what is this — he could make out that some creature, a bear, a wolf had come into the hall, some thing, some thing was roaring at them, grabbing at the boys. They were fleeing in his direction, the servers too, everything was rushing at him. Lamark stood. What is this? he cried out. Where is Emile? he said. Fetch the muskets, he shouted, and then whispered harshly, again, What is this? to Brother Jacquard at his shoulder. A light near them skewed and then went out and others followed and then it was hard to see anything, the only light the light from the high candles still remaining on the tables, reflecting gold like pirate trinkets, and then there was silence, and then an inhuman roar.

It was a beast, eight feet tall. It was a half-man with the head of an ibex or an antelope, and antlers above that spread out an arm span wide, with black lines and white on its long face and two long red bloody smudges instead of eyes, and this noise it made was ungodly. Its long arms swooped left and right like lizard wings as it clawed and grabbed at boys running past to its left and right. Each time it stopped and swooped the webbing draped under its long limbs spread out again and fell again, but it only stopped for a moment and then swooped clumsily again: and now gradually, step after awkward step, its buckles and armour grinding noisily, its brush-like brown fur sticking out at its high hips, it was approaching him. The little boys were passing fancies, they were snacks. It was looking straight towards Lamark and Robideaux, who alone who had stayed at the head of the table. The Brothers and Fellows had disappeared, Hucket too. Lamark made the sign of the cross. The huge fire at one end of the hall had gone out — how? — and the whole great room was filling with smoke. Buckets! called Lamark. Sand! No one listened. No one did anything he said.

Jacquard shouted from the door behind. He has defeated the Founder! Jacquard yelled in sheer abject fear. Lamark went closer to him, still watching the animal, still watched by it.

What is happening? Lamark said.

Had the choir started singing *now*, two hours late? Or was it that he heard one sharp high note sung out by a hundred young voices?

It is the wendigo, called Robideaux, still at his place at the empty table. The eater of souls. He has followed me from Quebec.

You brought it with you! screamed Jacquard.

It had a grey beard, Lamark saw now, hanging down from its bloody mouth, almost like chainmail hanging over its throat.

Why are they running, why is it here?

Jacquard was speaking at a rate: The Founder always wins! It is but a joke, a rite. One year it was a golem. Once he was a wooden Trojan. But now he is a — I do not know what he is … Something has changed. If the Founder is defeated, it fights the Procurator for the College. You must fight it! It was an old rite, it was never supposed to —

Are you absolutely mad?

Lamark realized he was gripping Jacquard's plush robes and let him go. Jacquard took another step away.

He comes into the hall for his tribute, Jacquard rasped. His voice came through wood dust. How can you not know this? Did your predecessor not tell you? He wishes to take us over. He wishes to take your place. He will take the youngest of our boys. The ten youngest. You must save them! You must save us.

We are men of God, Jacquard.

And then to Jacquard's burbling Lamark said, Give me your cross. He had taken his own off in his rooms as he dressed and forgotten to put it back on. Was that why the beast had come?

Jacquard pulled it over his shoulders and dropped it into Lamark's open hands, and then he pushed Lamark back out of the doorway towards the centre of the hall so as to shut the heavy bright door. Lamark turned to hear the beast's hoarse breath, the whimpers of the children, and the trees outside groaning and giving way. He looked into the dark.

The monster approached once more, taking huge stumbling steps, half loping and half creaking, and each of those steps made an echoing clomp that resounded off the walls and redoubled. Lamark could feel himself breathing, his chest like a man o' war rising and falling. He heard the boys, coughing and crying and lunging to escape in the far shadows. And mouth open to the acrid bright smoke, he caught a sob in his throat too.

He grabbed a long carving knife from the table. He stepped forward, trapped in a dream. Ten feet away, the beast stopped, swooped one arm round and over its shoulder, roared its high screeching roar again, and leaned forward again, like the goat in heat, like the Oriental dragons Lamark read about late at night in his rooms, secretly, when he was supposed to be making his devotions, but long-armed, unlike anything he had ever imagined, black now, white now, wearing its tattered black rags like a leper kept far from other men, with armour made of wood planks strapped upon its chest, things that it had gathered in long green talons in the woods and villages, things that it had kept and pressed to itself.

Lamark desperately tried to remember his training in exorcism and how it might apply for this situation and realized that it did not apply at all. The monster craned its neck up to the ceiling now, and it briefly tottered, but then it looked down, at him, angling its luminous beast's skull slightly right. One black claw rose as if to grasp him, as if to grasp him within, as if to lift him to its mouth and hold him and suck away his essence between its wet scuffed forehands.

Lamark felt himself take a step forward. He heard the words of the Lord's Prayer, and then realized it was him saying them.

If thou hast come, otherworldly being … he said. Then he was saying that the Lord was his shepherd. But then he felt himself pushed to one side.

Don't put yourself in danger, Robideaux, Lamark shouted, grabbing at Robideaux's shoulder, but Robideaux freed himself instantly and with utter physical grace. Lamark fell backwards, and he scrambled on backwards until his spine was hard against the reassuring wood-panelled wall.

The antlers shifted, following the movement, two points pointed up, two more. The beast roared again, as if in delight.

What is Hucket's *Technic* to deal with this? Lamark suddenly thought, madly.

Be calmed, demon, called out Robideaux. I am with you.

Do not fight it! Lamark shouted, as it roared again.

I am with you, monster, Robideaux called out earnestly. Stay, wendigo. Come.

He reached for Lamark's Habsburg cup from the table. He uttered a stern prayer in a foreign language. When he spoke again, his tone was as resolute. Please let's not break that, Lamark thought.

Sit with me, demon, he said. You are invited! Join us, please. For I know you what you are. I know whence you come.

Lamark felt the beating of his heart bursting at his ribs, as when he had seen the rabid panther in the village zoo watching him, knowing him, its beast's mind envisaging him torn to scraps; but now he felt his heart slow. The monster stood still. It was built for fighting, not disputation, born wearing armour, a hellspawn that had never known love. It angled its huge long head to the left as it listened.

The monster angled its head now towards the other side. It took one huge step rotating right, as when Lamark had seen the old innkeeper and his wife through the window at Le

Sanglier dancing to the quiet viols in mid-afternoon, privately, and then returned.

Tell me, wendigo, said Robideaux, curiously, tell me why have you come to me again. Am I to go with you? Is that my path?

He was holding Lamark's beautiful porcelain teacup up towards it, like a new housemaid. He turned the doubled black eagles to face the creature. His fingers did not shake; he did not spill a drop. Whatever pain in his hands this caused him, he was fixed.

Have you come to take me back?

He took a step forwards towards it.

What is your hunger? What is your need?

In his left hand Lamark was holding, he noticed now, the pages of his speech, with its I, and thou, and God's grace, and surely we are blessed. They were crumpled. They were torn. He closed his eyes. He didn't want to see Robideaux beheaded here, in his hall. He didn't want to see the beast lift Robideaux in his two great claws and drink what came from within, hot blood pouring down its wooden chest from its long jaws. He didn't want to; he couldn't bear it. Did he scream? He must have. And then he must have stopped.

He opened his eyes when he heard the first noise. A quiet birdlike cackle, a tittering.

Robideaux was still there, as whole as life.

What? said Robideaux, as if in response to something. There was a softer sound in the hall now around him, a warmer atmosphere. There was more light. Someone had opened a window at either end, perhaps. The smoke was clearing, quickly, so much so that the portraits of his predecessors were visible again, a rigid jawline, a bulbous nose.

The beast raised its great thin arms upwards now, brushing one of the beams. Then it lifted its skull right off its head, antlers and all.

The Lord preserve us, someone said behind Lamark, but then Lamark saw what was there, under the skull: Little Robert Argent, with a bewildered look on his face.

We thought we would scare you, Little Argent said from above. It's the story. It's tradition.

The beast kneeled, very slowly, and as it did it lowered Little Argent gently up over its bowed head with webbed arms, lowering its bloody gaze down as if ready to be blessed, and deposited him on the floor, the boy's bare little feet dangling until they touched wood. The monster's wings were but black cloth netting, Lamark saw now. It was made from pieces, like all of us. It had hessian and baize wrappings for a head.

After several moments blinking up at them like a toy stag, with some difficulty Little Argent undid the leather binding around his shoulders and lowered the enormous antlers into his grasp, softly, cuddling them as if they were his night doll. He looked for all the world like the wounded pelican, the baby albatross out of its nest, the warbler in the reeds, or some other one of the birds represented in glass in the chapel.

It was supposed to be a joke, he continued, in his heartbreakingly high voice. It wasn't my idea.

It's all right, Lamark told him, on his feet now, brushing himself down. He was still holding the knife with the thick handle. He put it down on the table top, with the tip pointing in.

Will Saint Matthieu House lose points? Brother Jacquard said we ought to do it. For japes.

You won't lose points, Lamark told him.

Jacquard was coming out now, smiling shamefacedly. The other Fathers were returning. Some of them snorted, some of them kept their distance. From their glancing and half-hidden smiles, Lamark could tell that they had been in on the joke all along, every man of them.

Robideaux, red-faced, breathing heavily, glow-cheeked and twitching, looked quite ready to stab the first person who spoke to him.

I see you with him, a voice rasped. I see how you look at him. For shame.

Lamark twisted to see Jacquard's face, all bitterness, inches away, all hate, pocked cheeks glistening, tiny black eyes fixed close on his own, this far away. He tried to free himself as Jacquard said, in his harsh whisper: I see all, and I tell the Intendant.

Lamark's heart beat now just as violently as before. He could not speak.

Jacquard sauntered back towards the back doorway where Emile and a young boy Robideaux didn't recognize stood, presumably Poignard's messenger, a slender young aristocrat holding his tidy horsewhip at his velvet pantalooned thigh, plumed cornflower hat looming over a face that was pale and shocked and amused and moving between these states moment to moment. Jacquard patted the boy on the shoulder as he passed, and he turned to follow, and then Lamark could picture Jacquard in the yellow salle holding court.

He swallowed the bile to calm himself, but it rose again, hot and worrisome.

The boys returned sheepishly from the sides of the hall. There was quiet laughter, but also more than a few of them were wiping tears from their cheeks. They were trying to obscure their fear, like the little men were. They were acting big, some of them, settling their shoulders, hiding what they had felt. Lamark uttered some soft platitudes.

The beast slowly continued unwrapping its rags, pulling wood planks off its chest, and Lamark could see it was a man's bony frame underneath, then a man's paunch. It was a tall man with a little boy on his shoulders that had created such terror in his heart. Just a man. And when the hooded black coat came off entirely, Lamark saw that it was Lawrence Hucket standing there before them, his strong mouth and jaws garishly lit up in the swaying lights that remained.

If you could see your face, Hucket said, with a grin.

*

Sitting close by to each other on the double seat in the Procurator's stuffy rooms, both of them lit up by adventure, after the sherry overlooking the Cloisters, after the Warden, bearing his green glass lamp on his stick, had sung out at the end of his rounds that all was well, still Robideaux could not hold his tongue. At last Lamark had to stop him, hand on his hand.

You are a good man, Lamark told Robideaux. But you have seen too much.

Do not speak to me as if I were one of your boys, Robideaux objected.

My task is to protect you. Please allow me that. If I have too much neglected you I regret it. It is because I have so many other cares under these roofs. But we must tend to you now.

Perhaps Lamark had had too much sherry this evening himself. But Poignard was coming the next day. Always the Procurator had something else just slightly on his mind. That was his burden. Always something just out of view, its warm breath in his ear.

He said I was a gift, Robideaux complained in a bitter, straight voice, looking ahead and then looking at Robideaux. You were there. He values my company. The things I have seen he wants to hear about, he says. He says he was stuck in his work, and I have given him new fire, but look at what he does with me! He toes me away like an old shoe, he forgets me. I asked him, do you not feel as a person feels? Do you know what it does to a person, to reveal their most vulnerable intimacies, and then to be cast aside? He reads out my love notes for his japery. He cannot say a serious word!

Please be careful, the Procurator thought, but he said nothing.

Even tonight, even tonight, with the wendigo, Robideaux began, and then changed course. We sat in Le Sanglier, Robideaux said quickly, as if he knew that Lamark must shortly stuff a napkin down his throat, bind his mouth, seal him up in the oubliette. The fiddles echoed off the stone walls. How warm it is there! Like this. They go on with their festivities in the village, you see, as we go on with ours here, as the Wendat go on with theirs, the Talapoins theirs, in their red monastic throne rooms with their black candles. It is human. We bury, we grieve. We are human! We spoke about the *Technic*. The songs in the tavern reminded us of human existence. Lawrence said to me, do you think this is what it is like to be God, to dream of metaphysics, while a song plays close by, and the humans rut in their sweat? To watch them. He has such thoughts.

I know, said Lamark.

He is not capable, Robideaux said, of attaching himself. He said to me, when he uses this word 'I,' it seems to call to his mind different associations than it does for me.

What?

He is not capable, he says, of companionship.

Be very careful, the Procurator thought.

Human companionship! He says, that when he uses the word 'I,' he means what is happening to him at a particular time. Nothing more. The queen and the chariot. You remember.

Nagasena's chariot, the Procurator murmured. Do you think he is ill?

Lamark was in fact relieved when Robideaux did not reply.

So you do not believe the Talapoin philosophy, Lamark confirmed: You trust in the continuous extension of your present and eternal soul in the eyes of God.

Of course! Robideaux spat. But then he looked terribly confused. He put his hands in his roughly shorn, mouse-brown hair. I thought they were . . . he began. I thought I was . . . he said. It would provide some escape, he said at last. He stood up and sat down again, in Lamark's blue chair now, looking utterly desperate. Lamark with his eyes traced Robideaux's black eyes, his hawk nose.

They listened together as the old bell toned sadly. Lamark pictured Brother Clifford with two hands on the thick tolling rope. Neither of them spoke. They listened to the sea breath in the willows. Steps passed in the corridor; the new stones of the building adjusted themselves and readjusted to the wind, to the cold. Then Lamark breathed in and leaned forward.

You have such gifts, the Procurator said tenderly. Such brightness. But you must tend to your soul also. There is a hospital at Bouges where you can —

Do not send me to that madhouse!

Lamark kneeled on the matted rug now, close by, almost falling as he did so. Let us pray, he said.

Hucket is not here, said Robideaux, like a man mesmerized. He stood again and paced the room, as if on a search. He is not anywhere. How can it be? He watches the barmaid pass, and he says, This is life. What is he? Not a person. Is he a god, do you think? He watches us all from a distance. He is so august. But what am I to him? He has sandals he loves more. He says, It would be madness, would it not, to always be the same. But I am always the same, with him, for him.

Lamark did not know what to say.

You must be careful, he repeated at last.

Robideaux was breathing heavily.

Keep your own company, said Lamark in a dead tone. Work in the gardens. For here we aim to cultivate and not run wild. He thought he should stand up, but somehow he couldn't find the moment.

He says he has changed his view. He *used* to have an I. He used to be a man. Now he is something else. He compares it to withdrawing oneself from another's warm body.

Lamark shivered. These men of the world, he thought.

You would think that would allow him to love, Robideaux went on, trying to spool out another of his ideas that would surely knot him once again. But the opposite is true, he says. He says that to love is to love oneself. But he cannot give himself: There is no one to give. How is it possible? If, and only if, he feels as I do — then I can go on. If not, I must die. I dream about him every night. He is here! In my head!

Robideaux's palms were pressed hard against his temples again. His sleeves fell, and not for the first time Lamark could not keep his eyes from tracing the design engraved there by the Iroquois: the dark tail, the fingers with mudded black nails, the cross-hatched, wide open, hideous mouth. Lamark again felt like he was kneeling in torrents of water.

Then he says his one great ambition is to leave no trace. To swim away like the silver dolphin. He never says a serious word! You saw him tonight. But how he thinks! Have you read in the *Technic*? You will. His ideas will change the world.

Their world, the Procurator said.

He is a different man in his books, said Robideaux, and then ruefully he added: He uses my life. The things I have told him. He takes them. He pilfers. It is nothing to him. You have seen. He gives me his sheets to read without a second thought, and I see myself quoted, scorned.

Go back to your tower, Lamark told him. You must rest.

Nagasena and Milinda, Robideaux said quietly.

He stood. Robideaux returned. They sat on the seat together again and said nothing. There was smoke in the air, embers, scents of the feast rising through the chimneys hidden in the walls. A vision came to him of Robideaux washed up from the sea, his clothes waterlogged, beard thick with sand. The sight came to him of Robideaux's body on the flagstones at the tower base, broken, blood washing out from every pore, his hands in the pond, ribbons of his blood gathering and parting in the black water. Perhaps he had dreamed it. What had Robideaux said about the Indians' dreams coming true? He felt his heart would crack, here in his chest.

Sometimes a baby whale with human eyes and forearms washed up on the shore. Sometimes the fishermen came from the village dragging a mermaid caught in their nets, snaggle toothed, her green hands still tightly clasped around her jewelled sword. They presented these wondrous damned things to the College, not knowing what else to do with them. They could not be thrown away. Could they be blessed? All marvels were created by God, were they not? All damnations too. It was a strange and wondrous world. All was not known. Who had made him the arbiter? Why did he have to weigh, what was kept and venerated, and what was thrown back? What if he said no?

You must be careful, Lamark said, half to himself.

This was their third interview. Poignard was coming the next day for his decision.

And Lamark still had the spirit in him from the night's events. Was it this that led him to act the way he did, he would wonder, in later years. Was it the humiliation? Was it the sour raspberry mousse, the absence of music? Perhaps, he would think later, he made his choice because it was the easier one. But was easier better?

Say a Hail Mary, Lamark said absently. Look to your soul.

I have been in Paradise already, Robideaux replied. It is a land far away. There is no mine or thine there.

You must not return, Lamark told him. It will be your death.

I cannot live, said Robideaux. To be made much of, and then cast away like a stone. This suffering. It is too much.

It was to his later regret that the Procurator reacted as he did. But he wanted there to be no whiff of scandal.

You have been all over God's great earth, he said scornfully, and this brings you low? An atheist and his sin? What of your vows, Robideaux?

Robideaux said nothing for a while, staring down at his ruined hands. Then he told the Procurator how he had come to join the Order. A second son, overlooked. Marked out by his intellect. But what he had always wanted was to see life, that was all. The story, he supposed, was not unfamiliar.

Let us speak honestly, Robideaux said, like men before God. Not all who joined the Order, he supposed, were entirely called. Did the Procurator himself never wonder about the path his life had taken? If he had chosen well—if he had chosen at all? A young man chooses, but another must shoulder. An older man pays the price. Another will be buried, in a Jesuit grave.

Work in the gardens, Lamark told Robideaux. Stay away from the shore. He laid his hand on Robideaux's shoulder. Robideaux leaped up as if startled, and then once again, in an instant, he was gone, the door gaping open behind him.

224

Who among us knows how to live, the Procurator wondered. Do you not see me? Am I here? Do I not have a mind? Am I not then worth speaking to? I met a man, Lamark wanted to say, and found myself an utter mystery to him.

Stay, monster, he said to the dark, still later that night, wrapped in his sodden bedsheets, suddenly sitting up. Stay in my rooms. No one need know.

And then even later still: Take me with you to Quebec. To Quebec, to your wild places, your wildest. For we are brothers. We are twinned.

*

It was to his later regret that the next day Lamark wrote to Poignard, who had not come after all, that it was his view that Robideaux had recovered fully from his experiences and should be sent back to New France. Poignard's secretary must have absently acceded. Robideaux was sent for within days. Some months later, far to the west of Quebec, Robideaux was tortured to death and became a martyr.

And so it was some months later still, the morning after that news came, very early in the day on his walk to Matins, that Lamark saw a small boat on the water. The sea was a grey mess that day, like a study for a painting in an underdeveloped, new and emotive style, one not yet invented, and the skiff rose and fell back down severely. He saw the man guiding it and recognized him at once, but was too far away to make out his

225

expression. When his arm went over his face, it was possible, or even likely, perhaps, that Hucket was simply brushing away the salt spray.

Cases like this do transpire, Poignard wrote to him. You did what you could. It was not enough. You will learn. You must always and at all times display exemplary care, he wrote, or dictated, was represented, in the enormous red letters, as if speaking already on behalf of some higher arbiter. I will make no further recommendation.

From the first day Lamark took over his post, the Intendant Poignard had not set foot in the College. His promises to do so came less frequently, and then ceased.

Lamark told himself, in later years: When I was young I was not yet the man I am now. And then wondered if he was squirming away from a genuine moral assessment of himself. He preferred not to think about such things.

*

When the snow falls, as it is falling now, one cannot but see the College differently. The deer that wildly come and go as they please in other months step more carefully in winter. The keepers burn little fires on the ponds in order that the villagers may come in and fish and not go hungry; and then, for a day, they have charge. The air is heavy with the smell of huge cloves of garlic roasting, such monstrous things. The Procurator and the other Fathers must keep their distance from the revels; they step more carefully, also. He is at the head of this place today as he was then. He worked on the physical structure of the College with Tams Argent for many years at his side. Now he works with Argent's son Robert, who still sings beautifully. The older boy died of plague. The buildings and grounds have been transformed under his care. They have just finished their latest improvement, the creation of a maze.

Some might say perhaps that I have not advanced, thinks the Procurator. That I reached my proper station. That my rise came to a crashing halt. I would say that if my life narrowed, it also deepened. I favoured action. What did it give to me, now that they are all dead? But why did I not send *Hucket* away? the Procurator wonders.

Sometimes a light will shine into your life, the Procurator thinks. It is like a rent, a tear in the sky. A brightness unlike any other. It is like the light of the stars themselves, seen from above our world. If you are lucky, it is God holding a lantern over you for you to see. But you must be careful. You could be wrong.

As he walks, the Procurator sees again Robideaux and his wild beard, crouched forwards in his rooms in the light blue chair he still has, tattered and patched as it is, staring back at him; then he sees Hucket in his boat, cutting through the waves. He wonders what he has built. As the grey waves crash, snow falls over them and into them. It cannot collect, so why does it fall?

Lamark sees again the salt water dappling Hucket's cheeks, his hands. Hucket had a way of remaining unaffected, the Procurator reflects. Was that his *Technic* after all? Robideaux was never spoken of. His death was seen as a kind of self-serving obscenity.

At the Feast that night, when he rises with the boys for the grace, he feels a sudden momentary dizziness and rests his hands on the table. The youngest boy leads them in Latin. This time, Lamark is not sure of his name.

Procurator Lamark has invited the scholar from Oxford who waited for him all afternoon to join him at table, and this rotund man is hungry for Hucket gossip, Lamark knows full well. But the Procurator says he is feeling his age. He tells the Englishman that he will need to leave early and retire to his rooms. Sometimes a storm from the sea will sweep over the College, he says, gathering up its strengths over the grey bare ugly ocean to break hard over his roofs and towers and confounding all, like a visitor from far away, something unbeknownst and quite unexpected. They can speak tomorrow, he says, perhaps. Once it passes.

HANDCUFFS

A path. A pond. **LAURA** *is sitting on a park bench, her long legs crossed under a topcoat in the spring cold, the very occasional fat smattery flakes absorbed one by one into the fabric. It's warm in the sun, it's cold in the shade. She watches the blue jays heavily come and go. Under her medical mask, her cheeks rise in a smile, as she wonders what the man she is waiting for is thinking.*

A cloud obscures the sun; the world grows darker. Dim the lights down low, I mean. But keep a spotlight on her. Throw her face up on the screen behind so we see her twice. Bright earrings. But she's tired. What does she do? She has her own production company.

MIKE: (*He's a little younger than her. He's not a problem to himself; that's what Laura likes. He is calling, entering from stage right, carrying a hockey stick in one hand, his hockey bag over his shoulder, like he's just come from skating, by himself, because that's all you're allowed to do these days*) Sorry I'm late. Sorry. Sorry.

Oh, he's a physio. Actually he's her physio. Good with his hands. Because that's what Laura likes.

And then it's like he suddenly catches himself, apologizing one more time, much more quietly, then stopping. And then he sits down on the bench next to her. Nustles the stick between his legs. He waits a while, and then he can't wait any longer.

MIKE: Hey there.

LAURA: (*Looks over, says nothing*)

MIKE: Pretty here with the ducks.

LAURA:

MIKE: I come here a lot.

LAURA:

MIKE: I love the ducks. But I feel like I've never seen you here.

LAURA:

MIKE: You come here a lot? To feed the ducks?

LAURA:

MIKE: It's peaceful, you know? I need to be outside. So long as you stay six feet away. (*Chuckles. Looks down at the bench space between them*) Length of a hockey stick. Of course, different ages, different heights. Junior A. Triple A.

LAURA: (*Still hasn't looked at him*)

MIKE: Steve wouldn't let me go. He loves me. He has separation issues. He wants to come out, whenever I'm out. He was throwing himself at the door. I thought he'd dislocate his shoulder or something. He thought I was taking him for a walk I guess. But I wasn't. That's not what I got planned for today. Not at all.

LAURA: I just got here.

MIKE: (*Looks up at her sharply, relieved perhaps that she's spoken, that he's not in the doghouse, so to speak*) Do you remember that time you came to my place?

LAURA: (*Because of her voice you can tell that she's grinning, under her mask, at the memory*) He went crazy.

MIKE: I had to lock him in the bathroom.

LAURA: I thought he'd hurt himself. His withers. (*They both laugh very softly*) I want to be my cat.

MIKE: Your cat?

LAURA: I'd sleep. I'd lie on the carpet in the front hall. I'd wait. If someone had a snack, I'd have a snack. I'd sleep some more in some interesting place. Anyway it's no problem. I just got here.

Sometimes she adjusts his collar. Sometimes he has chocolate on his lip, and she'll rub it off. Today, he holds his fingers out, and she rubs her cheek against the back of his glove.

MIKE: (*A little twitchily*) So how are you?

LAURA: Really?

MIKE: Really.

LAURA: Oh boy. Okay then: Fine.

MIKE: El husbando?

LAURA: He's fine. Promoted. He just got promoted.

MIKE: Sweet.

LAURA: Yes.

MIKE: And the kids?

LAURA: Wonderful. Safe. That's the main thing. (*Then, with no little pride*) Leslie got an A on his diorama.

MIKE: The dam?

LAURA: Wetland.

MIKE: Gotcha, wetland. (*Pause*) Happy Easter by the way.

LAURA: Oh you too. Happy Passover. (*Pause*) Our kitchen table became a wetland. He did it on Zoom.

MIKE: Everyone's safe?

LAURA: All safe. Want to go?

MIKE: It's early.

LAURA: We could walk.

MIKE: Do it up.

> So they do, they walk. **MIKE** leaves his hockey bag under the bench; he's not sure about that, but he doesn't know what else to do with it. But he brings the stick. He bends out his right elbow like a gentleman, and she puts a curved arm out, but they're six feet away from each other. Maybe the scenery changes behind them? They're walking through the park. On treadmills, or the stage turns as they turn? They have their routes, but they try to vary them. She left baby Amy at the drop-in with Bryan. She's supposed to be running errands. Trying to get toilet paper. Seeing her physio.

MIKE: Can't we take these off? I want to kiss you.

LAURA: I haven't been able to go to the hairdresser.

MIKE: Yeah everything's closed.

LAURA: I just want to be able to get my hair cut.

MIKE: I want to kiss you.

They look to the side and look around and step closer to each other, step back, step closer, their faces approach one another's like that painting of the people in bags kissing, Magritte? Their masks kiss.

She starts them off walking again. Closer to the pond again. Their usual route. Over there are the train tracks. You can see the containers, huge like Lego. Maersk and Canadian Pacific. She's always a step ahead. She's a little taller than he is.

MIKE: It's been bad these last weeks.

LAURA: Look, it's been horrible.

MIKE: I've missed you.

LAURA: Hmm.

Now they stop. Now they lower their masks. He comes towards her, and she holds onto the hockey stick and then pushes him away with it. He grabs it back from her. Then they raise their masks again. Then she walks on. He lingers. Then he follows.

MIKE: Is it three yet?

LAURA: I was early.

MIKE: I was too.

LAURA: It's not even close to three.

MIKE: What do we do?

LAURA: Take another turn?

MIKE: Let's get lost. In the woods.

LAURA: Yes then years from now some girl cheats on her school cross country and finds our bodies, and she's scarred for life. Steeping under the wet leaves.

MIKE: Exhumed.

LAURA: (*Thoughtfully*) We'd be canonized.

MIKE: Preserved in peat. Like that neolithic dude. But we'd have our arms around each other.

LAURA: They could still call it. Numbers are going up.

MIKE: They're not going to call it.

LAURA: It's like every time you get close ... (*Trails off*)

MIKE: They won't call it.

LAURA: Yes but ... (*Trails off*)
   So they walk on.

MIKE: Hey now would you look at that. Red squirrel with a black tail. What's he doing?

LAURA: Yes.

MIKE: Sign of spring.

LAURA: "If winter comes, can spring be far behind?"

MIKE: Sounds legit.

LAURA laughs just a little.

MIKE: Wait, what did you say?

LAURA: I don't know.

MIKE: At least someone's taking care of his nuts.

LAURA:

MIKE: (*Walking on*) Come on.

Sometimes it's hard to hear each other through the masks. Also, will the audience even be able to hear them through the masks? They might need to be mic'd up. Anyway, he doesn't know what to say. He looks around, looks left, looks behind. He takes a step towards her. She takes a step back. Keeping the distance. He keeps the stick flat between them, so as to judge.

MIKE: (*Snappy, frustrated*) How are things with you?

LAURA: I told you.

MIKE: About him. About them. What about you?

LAURA: I told you. That's me.

MIKE: Like what about your boyfriend?

LAURA: What?

MIKE: Your boyfriend.

LAURA:

MIKE: (*Probing*) Your lover. Your man. Your extramarital. Your love life. Your lover. How are things with him? Your mister.

LAURA: My mister?

MIKE: Last night when I was a little high it came into my head. Like mistress. Your mister.

LAURA: (*Savouring that*) My mister.

She licks her lips. Under the mask. It seems MIKE's got sides to him. And it's a whole different side of her. People are different, with different people. That's probably for the best. What are you like with your friends? What are you like with yourself if you spend a week utterly alone? Who are you when you're half asleep in a meeting, attending in class, or lying on your back, on the floor, fucking some guy, drifting in and out of the feeling, who are you then?

LAURA: Well. Oh boy.

Yes, she likes this. He dangles out the stick to her, and they hold on to an end each. They circle, they twirl. Then she wrenches it from him.

LAURA: He's fine.

MIKE: Just fine?

LAURA: Fine is okay. Really fine's not so bad these days. The only thing is —

MIKE: What?

LAURA: If I had one complaint ...

MIKE: Hit me with it.

238

LAURA: (*Over him*) He talks too much.

MIKE: Come on.

LAURA: Really. Too much talk.

MIKE: Come on.

LAURA: Really. Too much talk. Not enough of the other stuff.

MIKE: (*Genuinely surprised*) Whodathunk? Huh? He talks too much.

LAURA: I know.

MIKE: So what are you gonna do?

LAURA: About?

MIKE: (*Amused*) This problem you have. About this dude of yours not being able to keep his goddamn mouth shut for like two seconds.

LAURA: Well you see luckily I have a plan.

MIKE: Sweet.

LAURA: It calls for a rigorous program of discipline.

MIKE: And this program of discipline —

LAURA: Yes.

MIKE: What does it consist in exactly?

LAURA: Well I'll tell you. It consists in ...

MIKE: Yeah?

LAURA: It consists in ...

MIKE: ?

LAURA looks around.

LAURA: Whips.

MIKE: Oh yeah. Get the whip out, stop him talking. I like it.

LAURA: When he talks too much he gets the whip.

MIKE: Shut him up. Whip him into shape.

LAURA: And then what do you call it? Cat o'nine tails.

MIKE: I like it. I like it a lot.

LAURA: (*Silently*) He's on his knees in our hotel room, that's the place we go to, no he's on all fours. (*MIKE assumes these positions.*) And then he gets the whip. Then he gets the cat o'nine tails. And then he gets the riding crop. Then he gets the cane. (*She does all this with the stick.*) I'm raising marks on his skin. In my jodhpurs. (*She puts on a pair.*) Like an aristocrat. Because that's a thing he likes. The exploitation, because he grew up poor. This is what he wants, so I do it. I know all the mechanisms of control. I grew up with them. Anyway, I'm leaving lines, thick and thin. His mouth is gagged, you see, because of the talking. That's the point of this. And each time he makes a noise he gets another slap with the cane and I raise another welt. (*She does this with the hockey stick.*) I don't want to do it especially but it's what he wants. And it's a vicious circle, because he gets whipped with the strap for each noise he makes, but every time he gets strapped with the whip, he lets out another whimper through the gag, so I do it again. Because he talks too much. And what we've agreed on is silence. But what we get is whimper then welt then whimper then welt. Paradoxically enough. I find I want to hurt him. Part of me wants to hurt him. And he loves it. Paradoxically enough. This strong man. He's on all fours, at the end of the bed, in a studded collar, and I walk him around on a leash. I parade him around our hotel room, and I film it for all his friends and relatives, I livestream his humiliation (*this she does*), just to silence him. I'm enjoying myself now. I put fox ears on his head and I ride him around the room with a polka blasting out from my phone. I heat a poker in the fireplace and I brand him with the iron because now he belongs to me. He has my initials on his thighs now, one on each. That's forever. I make him strange. (*All acted out with the hockey stick.*) I do it all. Anything you can think of I do. In our hotel room. At three. He belongs to me. I stick my vibrator halfway up his ass, and I tie his ankles to the bed feet. I make him collect his own stringy threads of shit in a bowl. I make him scrape it off my dildo with a plastic fork. I rub his lips in it; I force his nostrils into it. (*Show as much of this as you want to. You can hide her apparatus in the trees. She reaches for each object as she needs it.*) I turn him around and I squat on his face; I shit slowly into his mouth. He loves it and he calls me his queen. And so I hit him again, because he's not allowed to address me. I've tied him down. He's weeping. He weeps. It's what he wanted. It's what we wanted. (*Has anyone walked out yet?*) This is just part of it. This is just a taste. We just want to break through. Things are so fucking normal, otherwise. We're locked down, otherwise.

*They return to their walk, stand up, unembarrassed, or maybe
a little embarrassed. Breathing heavily. Sweating a little. They
stow things away in the trees. They take their time.*

MIKE: (*As if part of him were somehow aware, still there, but also
responding to the last thing she said, Cat o'nine tails*) You're my queen.

LAURA: (*Complaining*) No one's allowed to do anything.

MIKE: That's what makes it fun. Being here. Being outside.

*She stops and draws her mask down and comes very close now.
She pulls him towards her with the stick. They are very close
now. She breathes on his ear, where his earlobe should be, but
he doesn't have one. Something happened when he was small.
She blows air around that diagonal. She traces the cut-off shape
with her tongue. Then pushes him away again.*

*MIKE takes a bit of time to recover from this. Long pause, to
recover. LAURA's fine, watching him. She drops the stick and it
falls with a bang, and she takes a few steps away. After a little
time he picks it up, takes a few steps with it, twirls. Then he
leans on it, stands, takes his phone out.*

MIKE: No, they haven't called it. See? Check in at three.

LAURA: Unless conditions change of course.

MIKE: I want to be in that room with you.

LAURA: Out of an abundance of caution.

MIKE: I want that more than anything.

LAURA: It's a fast-moving situation.

MIKE: Fuck that, I don't care.

242

LAURA: Oh and wild hungry dogs. If the whips don't work.

MIKE: (*Jovially, back on phone*) What?

LAURA: Pit of them. In the washroom. Hidden under the bamboo mat.

MIKE: Oh yeah. The discipline.

LAURA: I know.

MIKE: You're a maniac.

LAURA: Their tongues are teeth, did you know that? They're serrated. They saw through wood.

MIKE: (*Still on phone*) I did not know that.

LAURA: I'm talking about the ducks.

She takes out her phone too and they're abstracted, apart now. Six feet apart.

LAURA: Did you know the Spanish word for handcuffs is the same as the Spanish word for wives?

MIKE: Hmm?

LAURA: Word of the day. If you say the word "wives," in Spanish. It also means handcuffs. I hate that.

MIKE: No.

LAURA: "What power may care in comprehending justice for the grief of lovers bound unequally by love?"

MIKE: (*Looks up from his phone*) What?

LAURA: Quote of the day.

MIKE: Wait, what did you say?

LAURA: "What power may care, in comprehending justice, for the grief of lovers, bound unequally by love?"

MIKE: (*Back on his phone*) They're updating shortly. Oh wait it says. No. Await further updates. It's a fast-moving situation.

LAURA: (*Looking up from her phone*) What power ... comprehending justice ... (*She trails off*) So?

MIKE: So what do they call manacles?

LAURA: I don't know. (*Whispering*) I love you. I tie you down.

MIKE: What do they call fetters?

LAURA: Handfucks.

An empty passenger train rumbles by at great speed. It's daytime, but you can see the moon. They can't talk for a while. They sigh in frustration. They raise eyebrows. They wait. Then it's suddenly quiet. She looks down suddenly.

LAURA: I thought these were leaves.

The lights change and we see that this whole time they've been walking through discarded medical masks. A carpet of blue. He flicks some of them away with the stick. It starts to snow again.

MIKE: No one thinks about the people who have suffered most in this pandemic.

LAURA: Hmm?

244

They walk on. MIKE gets an idea.

MIKE: There's cowgirl.

LAURA: Say again?

MIKE: There's cowgirl.

LAURA (*Cluing in*): Reverse cowgirl.

MIKE: There's oral.

LAURA: Obviously. There's anal.

MIKE: Obviously.

LAURA: There's fur.

MIKE: There's diapers.

LAURA: No way.

MIKE: There's fur.

LAURA: Said that already.

MIKE: There's spanking.

LAURA: There's paddling.

MIKE: There's hot wax.

LAURA: There's cold showers.

MIKE: There's showering together.

LAURA: (*Thinking of something else*) There's having a shower.

MIKE: There's choking.

LAURA: There's plastic.

MIKE: What about feet?

LAURA: Yuck. We tried feet.

MIKE: (*Remembering ruefully*) That went well.

LAURA: Don't remind me. What about a threesome?

MIKE: What about a foursome?

LAURA: What about a fivesome?

MIKE: There's watersports.

LAURA: There's water hazards. In golf. There's foursomes in golf too.

MIKE: There *is* golf.

LAURA: There's swinging.

MIKE: There's cock rings.

LAURA: There's firemen.

LAURA: There's nurses. And Belgians.

MIKE: Belgians?

LAURA: Yes Belgians.

MIKE: Belgians. Hmm. Yeah, I guess.

LAURA: Some people like Belgians. It's just a fact.

MIKE: There's what you most need. There's your most secret self.

LAURA: (*Not listening*) There's Belgian nurses.

MIKE: I guess there's Belgian chocolate too.

LAURA: There's what you'd never show to anyone else. Anyone but me.

> *She's looking at the ground. Geese fly over them, in a V. They watch the leader switch places with the first to its left, and they fly on through the grey.*

MIKE: (*Tentatively, as if not sure of an invitation*) Or we could do the lingerie today?

LAURA: It's just a little uncomfortable.

MIKE: It drives me fucking crazy, Laura.

LAURA: (*Instant anger*) Don't say that. Don't use my name. I told you. I fucking told you.

MIKE: (*Instant apology*) Sorry.

LAURA: We agreed.

MIKE: It drives me fucking crazy.

LAURA: (*Scornful*) With your limited imagination.

MIKE: (*Smiling about himself, while getting annoyed*) Yeah it's limited but you know what, that's me.

LAURA: I didn't bring the steamer trunk.

MIKE: What do you think's in my hockey bag?

LAURA: Clever boy.

MIKE: Torsolettes.

LAURA: Me or you?

MIKE: Can we do open-crotch boyshorts?

LAURA: My father ran a bra factory. First one in Ontario. So I know all the words. You can't shock me with the words.

MIKE: But can we?

LAURA: There's something called frottage, where pleasure is derived from friction with a certain fabric.

MIKE: But can we?

LAURA: (*As if talking to a child*) Fine.

MIKE: What else?

LAURA: You decide.

MIKE: Here's the thing: My girlfriend, my mistress, my lover, she's found the lockdown challenging. She may appear to be a respectable mother of two out for an Easter walk in her local park in her knitted hat and a black turtleneck. But it's under there, under the mask, that's where the real action is. You can just make it out through the fabric. And what's happening there is beyond leather, beyond baby dolls, beyond balconettes. She knew her hipsters from her halters when she was still in school. Some of the things she wears, they're illegal in this jurisdiction. It's her armour. That's what keeps me going through these long days all alone. The thought of her. It's her secret body. It's what she'll wear for me.

LAURA: This is why she has to shut him up.

MIKE: (*Losing the thread as he sees that she's distracted*) It's just, this is what she wears, when she engages in her program of discipline. Of discipline. Laura?

LAURA: (*Incredibly harshly*) I told you, don't call me that. (*Change of tone: softer*) What else?

MIKE: Sorry.

LAURA: (*Change of tone: softer still*) What else?

They stop. Hearts are pounding? She licks her lips under her mask. I was going to say she likes to hurt him, but you know that already. How do they say all these things? I mean, in what tone of voice? You'll have to imagine.

MIKE: (*Stopping*) You know I'm like — where's the goddamn pond gone to? Where are we?

LAURA: Everyone's inside. You're not allowed to do anything.

MIKE: Nobody in the off-leash. Tells you something. When I take Steve there it's a madhouse.

LAURA: You're not supposed to call it that anymore.

Above them, a sad duck flies back and forth, to its mate, away from its mate. Then it lands recklessly, coming in low and hard like a bomb. MIKE watches in amazement, then aims the stick at it as if it's a rifle. He wanders around. He buries the stick in the ground upside down as a marker, a sign post, a fixed point.

LAURA: You brought your skates. That's cute.

MIKE: It's all you're allowed to do.

He goes away into the woods. LAURA says very quietly, as he disappears, that she loves him. But she just mouths it; he doesn't hear. MIKE is wandering around, rustling in the bushes, coming in and out, on and off stage, putting his hand above his eyes, looking at his phone, doing the things that people do when they are lost, a little bit frustrated, a little bit exaggerated, maybe. LAURA speaks very quietly, watching him at first, then speaking to no one in particular.

LAURA: When you love when you love when you love. I want to leave my husband. For you. I want to leave my baby. She keeps me up at night, I don't deny it. Have you heard anyone say that, ever? For my body to live again. Can you imagine that? It's your scent, it's your sweat, it's you with me, over me, drowning me. There's something about it. It's not what I want, but it's what I want. There's something about this that words can't say. To be attractive again, not to die. To be an adult, not a milk machine. To be free. To live here in this moment, with you. With this dipshit. To live with his body. It could be anyone. It could be an eggplant. I'd be free. Yes, this is how I spent my mat leave.

She smiles. Then watching him, her mood is changing, as she envisages.

Rub rub rub. Lick lick lick. Thrust thrust thrust. Grinding away like fat old joggers, thinking of your sandwich and your pension. You shift a little to the left, you shift a little to the right. It's pointless today, it doesn't feel right. That's how it is sometimes. Is this what you gave everything up for? You buckle for him; he likes that. Shifted to the left, shifted to the right, like a baby on its mat, like a corpse in the morgue. Until something changes. His body or yours. Something changes. And you're in some other realm, for a second. But then it all comes back. And you start again. (*Pause*) And some days this is the story that you'll live and die for? (*Pause*) What am I doing here? (*Pause*) We laugh at the sad ducks living out their sad ducky lives, not able to think, following a pulse, because they don't know how to think. They live and we die. It doesn't seem fair. I don't want to have sex. I want to have a shower.

MIKE: (*Comes back to the stick. Calls out*) Down there. The pond. The orange boats. We double back, then it's left.

LAURA: Right.

MIKE: (*Chuckle*) Left. We'll get arrested for stepping off the path. Breaking curfew.

LAURA: (*Still in herself, her thoughts*) You can't do anything. Nothing's allowed. Where do you get your food? You can't go to the store.

Walking.

MIKE: It's something just to be outside. There's a Rabba on the ground floor of my building. Down the elevator. Up the elevator. So I'm eating a lot of popcorn. I don't see clients. I see you.

LAURA: I have kids. Leslie doesn't go to school. He's on screen. I shouldn't be here.

MIKE: Yeah how *are* little Bryan and little Bryanette coping?

LAURA: Watch it.

MIKE: I have a dog.

LAURA: I keep telling you it's not the same thing.

MIKE: Yeah well I need to take him for his walk you know. I go at three a.m. When no one's out. When I'm allowed. It's my hour of exercise per day. Otherwise I haven't left the condo.

LAURA: We shouldn't be here.

MIKE: You have kids. Where did they come from, exactly?

LAURA: Some girls like to do it alone.

MIKE: Some guys need to be with someone.

LAURA: Some ladies want to be dominated.

MIKE: Some men want to be reduced.

LAURA: But yes there's always bestiality: man's best friend. He doesn't talk back.

MIKE: Some girls like horses. You know, for the jodhpurs.

LAURA: I think when people dress up in fur they're being childhood stuffed animals again.

MIKE: You can get chemically castrated.

LAURA: You can reinscribe colonialism in the bedroom.

MIKE: With leather.

LAURA: With Belgian chocolate.

MIKE: Make yourself into yourself on your brand-new kitchen tiles.

LAURA: Bite into my lip. Pierce the ... What are lips made of? What's inside them?

What they say next they say to the audience, standing next to each other, looking out at the audience from the black stage. Snow falling harder now.

MIKE: Yeah because I walk under your window. At three in the morning. Every night at three in the morning I walk past your house. But the lights are never on. I need my fingers in you. It's your body. I live and breathe for you. Holding you above me. It's like nothing I've ever known. I drive across town for you. I'd bike across the country. You'd think that the baby would be up, one time, that you'd be walking around, soothing her, that you'd see me through the window, that you'd come down for a second, a minute, five minutes, and I'd press you against the wall, your side wall, and we'd fuck, standing there, without saying a word, pressed up against the side of your house, like monkeys with purple cheeks, the only thing in the world the scent of you, like one sparrow landing on another for its two seconds, blind-eyed. But you never are, we never do. This little doggy pushes against my shin because he wants to go home. He doesn't understand why we're out. But what's crazy is that it's not your body. You could look like anyone. You could be burned all over and scarred and ruined and I'd still want to eat you alive. I'd drink you down. There's something about this that words can't say. It's not the outside. It's the inside.

LAURA: I want your hands around my throat. I want you to squeeze. I want to die. I want you to drown me. In this tub. In this room. I don't care. Drown me, I'm that tired. I can't go on.

I want to live. I want to be an adult. Otherwise hold me under the water like a child.

MIKE: I want to weep. I want to be held. I want you to change me. Even if I were dead I'd still want to fuck you. Even if we'd drowned. Our puffy white skin and our lips like pillows. I wouldn't care. Even if everyone were dead.

LAURA: The lips the mouth and all the wet organs. My cunt my ass my scars. The outside of the body is dry. The inside of the body is not. Is that it? My elbows and my knees are dry. I want to do it for money. I want to do it outside. I want to do it in front of people. Would that make me love you? Wet and dry. There must be some way to stay alive. To feel like you're alive. If you could fuck me in my eye. In my heart. As if somehow that would be love. (*Pause*) I have never been this alone. But have I ever been this sad? (*Pause. Looks at him, on his phone*) Thrust thrust thrust. Like lick lick. Rub rub rub. Until something changes. But what if nothing changes? Except that you can die at any minute. In the most ridiculous unheard of ways. Because you *breathed* wrong. Because you swallowed wrong. Because you tripped off the curb at the wrong moment. And all this time you've spent, in your life, thinking about another person. Why?

MIKE: I want to tell you.

LAURA: I want to love you.

MIKE: I've never been so alone.

LAURA: I've never been so sad.

MIKE: Not being with you hurts me, fucking right here, every second of the day. I could never tell you.

LAURA: From the moment I walked into your exam room I knew I'd married the wrong man. I had a baby. When it was you all along, and we'd just never met, that's all. It doesn't seem fair. But what can you do?

MIKE: We have to do something.

LAURA: We're taking precautions.

MIKE: I hate this, what we do.

LAURA: It's demented.

MIKE: It's what we do.

LAURA: There's something wrong with me.

MIKE: Is there something wrong with us? You're married. You have kids. I have a dog. You say it's not the same thing.

LAURA: Whatever this is, I hate it.

And then as if they notice each other again for the first time, they turn and face each other, and their masks kiss again, and then they stop and separate, and she sobs briefly, and it's a horrible sound, and they part, distanced again.

MIKE: (*On his phone*) They called it.

LAURA: (*Instantly*) I knew it.

MIKE: We can move the booking. We can keep the points. But they called it. It's shut down. Because of the lockdown. (*Desperately*) Now what?

LAURA: (*Walking on*) Another turn.

MIKE: (*Summarizing from phone*) Now it's against the law for us to even be here: we're not from the same household.

LAURA: Can't we go to the clinic?

MIKE: (*Snitty*) The clinic's shut.

LAURA: Let's go to a place. Any place. My car. Come.

MIKE: Fat chance.

LAURA: Why not?

MIKE: It's, like, pathetic.

LAURA: (*Inviting*) Come *with* me.

MIKE: You say you want to. Then you pull your back out over the handbrake.

LAURA: I thought you could help with that. Behind the copse then. In the trees.

MIKE: With the joggers? It's fucking freezing.

LAURA: There's no joggers.

MIKE: There's a reason.

LAURA: Anywhere then. You say where.

MIKE: It's not about where.

LAURA: Seriously. We've been to places. What's wrong with a place?

MIKE: I'm not going to a place. It's not legal.

LAURA: (*Scoffs*) Legal.

LAURA turns to leave.

MIKE: I want to be able to see your face. I want the room. I don't want a tree.

LAURA: Keep calm and carry on.

MIKE: It's not enough.

LAURA: We're all in this together.

MIKE: It's not enough.

LAURA: Well I need to get back to my kids.

MIKE: (*Scoffs*) Kids.

LAURA: (*Very seriously*) Watch it.

MIKE: I want *all* of you.

LAURA: (*Crying out*) Don't you want to fuck me?

MIKE: I want to see your face.

LAURA: Since when do you even care?

MIKE: We're not even supposed to be here.

LAURA: Do you remember? We used to kiss.

MIKE: Yeah I remember.

LAURA: No one's allowed to do anything.

She takes the stick and hits the stage with it, hard and then lets it drop. And then walks on, and on. He picks up the stick and follows her and catches up, and they walk together.

Until now at last they are back at the pond shore in wet fall boots, both sets elegant. There's a little brick barrier at the end of the grass, water below.

An elderly couple walks past, eyes them dangerously, walks slowly on. When most people are just staying inside at this time. Following the rules.

MIKE remembers that he had a line in his head as he approached her: "You got away okay." But he forgot to say it, at the sight of her. Something about seeing her blanked his mind, blasted it, wiped it clean.

LAURA realizes that she left a bag of stale bread crusts she'd prepared for the ducks on the kitchen counter. Bryan might find it and wonder. She'd forgotten it until now.

There's nothing else to do. Nowhere else to go. They both sigh. There's a lot of suffering, and these are people who have it easy. So then this silence, it's very despairing. In this park, this park, of all places.

The silence.

The silence was very despairing.

It was a very despairing silence, and they despaired.

LAURA: (*In a voice that admits confusion*) So now what?

MIKE: (*In a voice that suggests he's given up*) Whatever you like.

LAURA: Hmm.

MIKE: Fuck, man.

LAURA: What's the point?

MIKE: Fuck.

They walk on for a while, careless, sad.

LAURA: It's killed something in me. These last few months.

MIKE: Something's died in me.

LAURA: I wonder what would have happened if we'd met at a different time. I'm at the sink. I'm changing a diaper. I'm thinking, What if we'd met at a different time? In a different place.

MIKE: Well, we didn't.

They stop for a long while then walk back in silence. Hold hands briefly; let their hands drop. Then they are back at their bench. They stand there for a long time too. He rests one hand on it. It's all you're allowed to do. He's happy that his hockey bag is still there. She's looking over at the hotel. The art deco neon sign breaks her heart.

On the screen in the background, show the first time they met here. They sat here so innocently. It was warm and he took his jacket off, and she took it and rested it in her lap. That seems like a long time ago now, when this started to change. They watch themselves as they were before.

LAURA: (*Sweetly*) Goodbye then.

MIKE: (*Sweetly*) So long.

LAURA: Stay safe.

MIKE: Stay safe.

LAURA: We're all in this together.

MIKE: I feel like it's impossible.

LAURA: I know.

MIKE: It's just the times.

LAURA: I know.

MIKE: If we'd met at a different time. In a different place.

LAURA: I know.

MIKE: Goodbye then.

LAURA: Goodbye.

He knocks the hockey stick upside down on the floor twice like a signal. She turns away, and so does he. They walk away from one another. She goes in the direction of her car. He swings his hockey bag back over his shoulder.

She stops.

LAURA: (*Hopefully, calling him back as he leaves*) What about pretending we don't know each other?

MIKE: Hmm?

LAURA: Pretending we've just met.

MIKE: I don't know.

They part again, walk away, stop at the same time.

MIKE: No. Yeah.

They come back to each other. He drops his bag. She touches his glove to her cheek.

LAURA: Like being picked up.

MIKE: On a park bench.

LAURA: There is that.

MIKE: I guess.

LAURA: Like spies in the Cold War.

MIKE: But where?

LAURA: Park bench.

MIKE: The place.

LAURA: The park.

MIKE: Okay.

LAURA: All right.

Pause. Three little ducks fly off again. They watch.

MIKE: Tomorrow?

LAURA: Same place.

MIKE: Tomorrow.

LAURA: (*Shaking her head*) Say, next week.

MIKE: (*Doubtfully*) Next week?

LAURA: Same time. Same place. Next week.

MIKE: Okay then.

LAURA: Until then. Unless the situation changes.

MIKE: Yup. For sure.

LAURA: (*Wistfully*) Can't wait.

MIKE: Me either.

> *They stare at each other for a long time.*

LAURA: Goodbye then.

MIKE: So long.

> *He leaves.*

LAURA: Goodbye then.

> *She looks at her phone, checks a few things, looks up. I love you, she mouths silently, under the mask, but no one sees or hears. She turns to go, and turns back.*

LAURA: (*Quietly*) Bring your dog, next time.

> *She bursts into tears, she weeps. She knows she's never coming back here. Not with him.*

LAURA: (*Shouting*) Bring Steve!

WITH
MILINDA

Bruce Chatwin, he wrote very beautifully refined travelogues, though mostly none of it happened, so we could put him in novels, I mean he also wrote novels, set in Africa, shall we put *The Songlines* in Semi-Fictional Travelogue? It takes place in Australia. English, of course, English, Eton, Sotheby's, that old world. I have boxes of Male English Writers About Australia, in the basement.

Down under!

Just joking.

These are our new shelves, pride of place. Different story. First things first.

Now Proust *Against Sainte-Beuve,* here now it's Proust's literary criticism, light blue glossy cover, they put Sainte-Beuve there, but you can't really take Proust seriously as a literary critic.

Doped up, medicated, cork bound the entire time, a morphine-addled insomniac dandified madman. You called *me* something like that once. Last June. I don't mind. He was a killer at heart, he had that cold eye. But he wrote like an angel in a patisserie.

We need a whole different section! Literary criticism, no, French literary criticism by novelists, no. Dandified Moustachioed Psychotic Literary Criticism by Murderers.

Yes, well, Althusser, say. He was a theorist. It's books by Franco-Hungarian Dandified Moustachioed Asylum Dwellers. Fortunately my sanity is intact. I'm just wondering with Skvorecky now —

god these are dusty my lungs my allergies now it's impossible to breathe here I'm standing here coughing kneeling coughing bent over this stupid strap IV pulling everywhere everywhere I go

— Skvorecky he's obviously Czech and round faced, somewhat pustulent, white hair, so I can put him in Bohemian White-Haired Swansong Literature (he adored jazz, it's supposed to redeem you, that kind of love), because he's not truly exactly specifically precisely a Canadian writer, but my section on Melancholy Czechoslovak Exile Literature of the Jazz Age is so thinned out

Once separated off I suppose. Well that happens, things fall apart out here in the countryside, there's nothing to bind you, only the fields staring up at the night like sleepless children. Only the two of you.

Just outside Guelph.

Ten years of the sun setting over the glory of the rapeseed

The Guelphs and the Ghibellines! I thought you'd like it. You always talked about the tiger in the rainforest. You used to. And the church is so close by for you. Spitting distance. Like us.

the moon, in June

coughing again but no, yes it's good to have them in my hands again, it's been too long, since we said, do you remember?

yes it's a terrible thing, a horrible thing.

God I want it to stop

stop coughing stop thinking stop talking yes no

I know.

I'll never work again, now.

Milinda, how did we both get so thin?

Yes my dear my darling I'll come to bed. This is very nearly done. Just a few more boxes.

Find some place for Lawrence Hucket.

I'll turn the music down then

Well it's like medications you can't just take them there has to be an order or else it doesn't work

Yes I remember all about your training I'm just comparing, I mean adducing

Well have some more gin. If it makes you feel safe.

No listen darling sweetheart for the last time I'm, I just, I want to be able to find a book of Love Sonnets by Austro-Hungarian Financier-Impresarios when I need to and no I haven't been up so long, I just came down to, it's the middle of the —

I *have* slept

well two, three days ago, I'm not sure

I *am* writing

after ten years of not writing

well maybe *you* should take a break if

what are you doing, no I don't want to *read* them, I'm trying to put them in order, the whole idea is to —

well yes of course women can write books too, if they must

No. All right. You're right.

I'm sorry.

Will you put that back, will you please?

If you can't sleep go back to sleep. I'll be quiet. I promise

Listen. Sweetheart.

268

Driving right from the mental hospital to IKEA, one madhouse to another.

I'm just joking. Don't cry.

Yes, you always loved your ruby earrings. Beacons of hope.

It's our new start. Now that I'm back. New life. New bookshelves. IKEA. Just like old times. I do like them. I love them. Just put it back.

I should call my daughter first, but who can blame her

Pulling it around pulling these straps with me everywhere I go. Like I never left the madhouse.

No Calvino goes in Italian Folktale Collectors not Mitteleuropean Logical Studies I mean why would he? My whole order is — the whole thing I'm trying to do is order these books in an intelligible —

If you can't keep things in order then how can you —

The world is irrefragably, yes resistantly, but we bought these shelving units (my fucking God that's a phrase shelving units) in order to —

No.

To do one last thing.

Because it's late.

when the books are in place

Then I'll sleep.

Because it took me so long to build them.

Fine, to assemble them. You can bury me in this one. Pour sweet meatballs over my body.

Oh I'm just — don't —

I'm sorry.

Do you remember at your door? When we visited Tuay Bareg? How you laughed. At the door with me, laughing. Your mother's gargoyle face frownscowling in the black windows above us. We laughed.

It's cold. I'm tired. Coughing all over. Give me some of that gin. Sit with me. Take a box.

You saved my life.

But I want it to stop

No I'm not growing a moustache, I just haven't shaved.

It's good to do this. So long in boxes I bet they feel they haven't lived for twenty years, don't they, like they haven't breathed. And look at you in your white nightdress! You look like one of your saints in a graveyard. Made of stone. Preserved by gin!

Oh I'm just joking. Look I have your Nora Roberts here snug up against my Philip Roth, quite a couple, no?

No, I don't need help, just put it back and wait until it's done.

Get this thing out of the way, out of me.

Not yet. We can do it now.

God, just let me put my arms around you.

Fine.

No, I understand. Just sit then. Pointless anyway with the pills. Over before it starts. And they serrate my skin. The same with work. No one will employ me now. I'll never work again.

Such a quiet night.

It feels like the time.

I'd like to visit my daughter first, my Cassie. But of course I terrify her.

And would you believe it? Tony Anschauer, wheeled into court to face his accusers. I knew him once. This is why I don't watch the news.

No I'm not being, you're being — will you. Stop! This isn't for you to — Because I have categories! Look at it it's Borges in English not Borges in Spanish so it goes in Refined Aesthetes of the Global South in any case not Blind Poets Who Loved Norwegian, you stupid, refractory bitch, don't you know any- thing? Have you ever even read a book? Do you know me at all? Do you want to help me at all? At all?

Sorry. I'm sorry. I've been up for so long, these books, these boxes, they're in no order, just things everywhere, dust, I can't. I feel so alone all the time so sad all the time they're my only —

There's no way to ...

With you being so ... with me being so ...

I don't want to. There's one thing I need.

Do you remember we were so happy that day, you in your terracotta-coloured dress. And your ruby earrings like Clytemnestra's beacons, matching your lipstick. We danced. Floating an inch above the waxed floor, laughing. No family, no friends, just us at the Intersteer. I lifted your brown veil. One strand of your hair I breathed through all night. When she saw the picture Laura said it looked like something had shat you out.

But somehow my books have all been in boxes for so long, I mean that has to mean something, doesn't it? You had me box up my books. For space. We agreed. So that we could breathe. Because I was sick. You said it was better for me to breathe. The country air. That it would be calmer. But to have everything sealed up for so long, unbreathing. Books in the basement, growing mould in the country cold, it's not right.

Do you know what the man in the next bed told me? He said that I'd never see you again, he said that you didn't want to see me, he said that you were the reason I was there at all. I mean can you imagine? He used to talk to me, after we'd had our plastic dinner and our meds, after the last lights out warning, the Haitian orderly used to laugh, her hands smelled of cocoa butter, rubber boots squealing their way down the corridor to death, and I'd put my pillow over my head, so as not to hear him. He said you were a killer at heart, Milinda. He said I was going to die soon.

No air, just ventilation, and bars on the windows. It's like an old schoolhouse. But several of them together. We sit on our beds and we wait for our meds. Never a candle, only a bright blue pill in a tiny cardboard cup. And me, staring at my hands, wondering whose hands they are. Staring at my wrists.

thinking about my childhood

day in, day out.

He said I'd never see my books again, he said you'd make me sell them on the street, out of a cart, in Budapest, he told me I'd never walk out of there, never go home again, every time you left he said it was the last time. All of us in bed the whole time like my father that time. Huge man with his grey shaved thatchy head. Talking bed to bed. I never knew his name. He ran his fingers around my scar, he said it felt like a daisy. He said you wanted a man who could build a bookcase, not a man who weeps all night over books he can't read anymore, because he can't concentrate, because there's something in his head, there's this voice in his head, all the time, because he can't recognize, because it makes no … He said you didn't feel safe.

Can you put that down please? I'm talking.

Milinda, how you could put me in that place

the dreams I had

Because I wanted to kill you. Because I wanted to kill me.
Because I had that cold eye.

Nothing to read there.

And every night there's nowhere to hide.

Nothing makes sense

Like I never left.

I don't want to.

This little leather box? I stole it from the orderly.

But God, I just want to have my arms around you, I need to
hide myself in you, it's all I've ever wanted.

Recently.

Will you put that down, I'm trying to say something! No sweetheart you don't have to — You make me so — will you put it
down? Because I have a system!

It's about forgiveness, Milinda. It's literature, it helps you know
people. God when you — when you leave me there, tell me,
what am I supposed to think?

I don't know: *Encased. Immured.* Why did you do that to me? To help me — what does that mean? To feel safe?

It's literature, not religion. It doesn't *quell.*

Of course you resist. But I have a system.

It obscures?

To feel safe

how it's been for you

I'd open a window to begin with. I don't care. Because I'm putting some fucking sense into things.

Oh fucking stop crying, Milinda. No will you just shut up and listen to me — I don't want to read anymore, I don't want to understand

Well what did you expect? I'm sick.

Because I need air. I don't want —

no sounds to carry. no one to hear.

Guelphs. Ghibellines. I have to ask you.

God I want it to stop

We *all* want to feel safe

Last June. The moon watching me. I was looking at my hands. Looking at my wrists.

Somewhere in these books, he said.

He said there was an answer.

He is wrong.

But you were a nurse. You know how.

Now would you believe that. On the radio. *Scissors and Stones.*
What are the chances?

Turn it off.

Please, let me put my arms around you.

My God, can I hide in you one last time?

Give me your hands. Don't cry. Don't cry. It makes me — you
make me —

It's me. It's in me.

fuck god this I just want to stop coughing

Here

please

look

You see? We're both crying now.

dusty

One more box. No more books.

Could you give me your hands?

Will you do this thing for me?

I can't read anymore

I don't know anymore

please

It will make us feel safe

we'll put some sense into things. Look.

it's midazolam

lidocaine

propofol

rocuronium

god they sound like planets

they sound like angels

like monks

like monsters

There's no smell anymore when your hair is in my breath
there's no scent anymore

nothing breathing anymore

It doesn't matter what the church says; we're our own church

And we have this IV already this strap it couldn't be easier

Of course you'd resist. It's your training.

First one then the other

But there's an order you follow

turn off this voice

it's the last one that does it

if you read the labels

if not we could mix them up

in my Habsburg cup

the lidocaine is just for the burning you see

the rocuronium is just to be sure

it's the propofol that does it

don't cry now

if you read the instructions

to keep them in order

they sound like angels

like monks

like monsters

but they have to be in order

or else it doesn't work

one after the other

you can make it stop for me

will you hide yourself in me

you can help me break through

if you kill this thing in me

will you make me die

LAUD WE
THE GODS

I am a man with a secret. It fires up under my ribs as I push my cart along. I am a man with a knife under his coat (there was a time when I kept a knife under my coat). I smile like a bachelor tripping down his latest conquest's steps. If the boys of the neighbourhood (the rough shells, the scamps) do not trouble me now — frying bigger fish — it is because they do not know me, not as a man with a secret. Sometimes it snows and my wheel hubs gum up; then the metal of my cart's handle is colder to the touch than a nun forgotten in a cavern. I push my way along as best I can, my books and my worldly possessions always in sight. My blue blanket and my broken Habsburg cup. Pushing this cart up and over small mountains of rubble, broken down wooden fencing that once upon a time was trees.

*

The boy said he'd found something I had better see. The others have jowly, sulphureous skin; but my boy is dainty amongst the banana peels and bomb craters. A slim hard face, and he fingered his knife as he spoke. The grip was decorated with ivory pictures of fox skulls. And yet he is a boy. They used to fall over their Latin pronunciation, their *-ibus* and *-imus*. He led me onwards. I wondered if there were more boys, more boys watching us from the broken windows across the way, pointing rifles.

*

When I was a priest, a million years ago, I was respected. The Gods are all in hiding now but I remember their faces. I remember the God with the Drooping Moustache, and the God of Staying in Bed. I am the one man in the world who knows them. Times have moved on, as our editorialists are fond of saying. I push my cart along and I keep the Gods with me: the Sad-Faced God and the God of Building Canoes. I stop to pick up pieces of postering. I pull chewing gum from my beard, when the mood strikes me. The boys in the neighbourhood throw boulders and pebbles and curse me, and I pray reverently to the God of Knowing My Own Mind.

*

First there was a bank. I wasn't happy leaving my cart outside, and I left it and walked back to it and left it and walked back to it, but he locked it up with the chain he kept around his waist. If anyone wanted to take it, they would have to carry it. Good enough, he said. The bank was a dusty wooden vault with green shades over tellers' lamps. Every teller's window was shattered, but they had left the shades, I don't know why. Smoke darkened the blinds long ago, it was terribly cold. I could imagine sportswriters working there. I mumbled something to the God of Hair. I saw the body of a rat, are we supposed to hate baby rats also? I wondered where the bankers used to take their lunches, naturally. Not the proles with their brown bread sandwiches, but the executives, the captains of industry. They built a tower over the branch. The boy said he wanted to show me something different. If you were my charge, I said, I would have kept you far hence; this is a treacherous place. His eyelashes were wet little ballerinas. I had a secret hope, of course. We all have our secret hopes, to keep us insane, just when we think we are starting to turn blue they pull us back into the magenta once more. He pointed to a gold ring in the floor. He asked me what I thought. I shrugged. He bent, all bones like an ortolan, and pulled on it: trapdoor. He got a board from a smouldering pile in the corner and rubbed a rag onto it to make it hot. He led me on.

*

When I was a waiter I likely served their parents. Perhaps I suggested, while knowing my place, the wine that served as the aphrodisiac spark of their getting. I was a waiter in some fine establishments, you see, in some of the finest establishments, and just today when I stopped to pick up a good long rectangle of corrugated cardboard for bedding, I thought of myself, in black bow tie, waltzing through the dining room with a bowl of walnut-scented gnocchi, peerless. My clients, my clients would ask the maître for me, especially. They took the same table each Friday evening. The wallpaper was embossed cream. Now their children beat me with broom handles. Though we believed in the same Gods. We were dying out then, we were all dying out, but I remember a whitefaced Duchess pulling me down towards her, gripping my forearm, for dear life, to whisper: *Mark!* And she would ask me: what do you know of the God with the butler? Such might be her concerns. The God they put on trial, have you heard anything? My clients, my clients knew that I had been a priest, hundreds of thousands of years before, and though it might seem socially awkward — or politically awkward, given the times — to ask, such was their devotion that they did ask. People with true manners can break the rules, from time to time, *because they do so with all grace.*

*

The boys live in tents in the vacant lots. They shit in rubble and eat cats. Memory is the gouger, and memory is the salve. I sing to the God of Foolishness as I walk, I joke with the God Who Murdered the Old Washerwoman. The boys wear bandanas and carry knives. They scream out scurrilous threats to my manhood, such as it is. I look for cans of food, and there are places where you will be given fetid soup. And there are people trying to be good, who wish to share, who will not send you away, at least until they tire of you. Sometimes I sit in my cart, when it is raining. I push myself under an awning and lick the washy rills off my cheeks, they taste of asshole. Sometimes I collect enough bottles to trade in for a delicious hot dog. Bubbles of grease collecting into lines. As I walk I keep my eye on the building pediments and I see the Gods perched on the roofs like hawks.

*

We were in one of the oldest temples. A place that was ancient before ancient things were conceived of. Murky air, the Egyptian smell, and sneaker and boot prints in the thick white dust. And we could feel the stone jut so slightly out where once there had been wood panels. My hopes welled again. How cold it was! Something moved against a wall to terrify me. My boy waved his torch at it. The God of Eels. I was full of the past: I could see acolytes kneeling in a row, I could think our rites were performed here, and here, and here, a million years ago. Tears welling? I wanted to thank him. Me, thank a boy, for bringing me to this place. The priest thanks the ephebe; all that is solid melts into air. He went away to the right. I regretted us making any noise at all, here, I breathed in our scent. His thin shoulders, the two of us in the crypt: Sandro and me in the wine cellars, the night I was fired. Then in the dark, in the burning shadows, he showed me a golden bird — and I lost my breath. We were silent. It is a great and powerful God, I murmured, unsure of myself, unsure of my judgment. Can it do anything, he asked me. His red and black unsmiling mouth. He said: I knew you'd tell us if it was worth anything.

*

My position had become if not unsafe then at least unsavoury. There was a sense of the best of times having passed. The Gods had sanctified my clients, the Gods had layered the world into sponge and icing. What mulch would follow their departure? My clients were anxious. I leaned in closer. Whispering, quickly, so as not to be seen: The Gods cannot be harmed, I told the wealthy. Do you think the God of the Twenty-Four hours is mortal? The God of Cunning Tribes persists, I told them. Full of hope they would watch me roll out the desserts.

*

When I was a priest I caressed these heads. I trained them. I was a man in charge of boys. I took my work seriously because I knew that I was one of a long line, and I knew that these boys would one day become men, and would need a code and an order tucked inside them, a map gradually unfurling in the esophagus. I led them in rites and songs, their parents trusted me. Parents brought me their most prized possessions, their boys. They came to my temple and left them with me with a solitary instruction: Mould this wet lump into a man.

*

One of the boys has curly hair. Another's locks are lank and soft as an otter blanket. One of the boys has studs in his eyebrow, this is something I do not condone. Mine is a soft one, he is less of a criminal. When the five of them chase me down the alley and kick my cart over and stamp my bedding into icy puddles and try to set fire to my cart and leave me bashed and bleeding I sometimes feel he is acting more half-heartedly than the rest, or at least thinking of hanging back. I focus on him, his gritted teeth. If you had come into the Doré, I'd have brought you a strawberry nectar. Not from the menu, something special from André, especially for the young master. Say this to yourself as you count your teeth with your cut tongue and moan. On the journey home, after dropping him back at school, the mother would say to the father: What a good, kind man Mark is. We must remember him at Christmas. And the father, sitting behind the driver, nods. The same quick nod as his boy. Reading the editorial page. With half a sirloin for the young master. Half a steak for the God of Steaks. I tell him about the God of Flight.

*

I sit in the sun and sing and fart: the Gods pray to *Me*.

*

When the policemen last brought me in, they fed me gruel. My cellmates beat me with the plastic tray. So the policemen kept me apart. They had their orderlies wash me and so I saw my privates. They gave me a new pair of pyjamas. The inspector was a woman. I came about, I came to, they sat me in a chair. She told me that the problem was not that they could not find the perpetrators; what I was describing was not considered a crime at all. So she had no choice but to let me go.

Three times until it came he wrenched at the bird and then lifted it off the wall. He brought it to the dusty table we'd pulled into the middle of the room. The boy stepped back, and so I began, knowing that I was full with the God of Returning to My Place in the Temple. And if I did not remember the precise detail in its precise configuration, still I was in the place with the altar and the wafer and the helping hand. I moved my hands across the bird. I spoke to the winking God of Deathbed Renunciation. I broke off. I told the boy: We perform the rite to step into the God's world, away from our own. We must needs be calm, if we are to succeed. It is best done at nightfall, I told him, but here we can forget both the sun and the moon. He spat on the floor. What's a rite, he asked me. I began again; I moved my hands over the bird and said what words I could. Here was sweat on my forehead, sweat in this cold place. I thought I saw the bird spread its wings, but it stayed where it was. The boy was playing. He rested his knife blade on the ripped fabric over his thigh, I could see the naked skin in the torchlight. I said to the boy: Come closer, I need you, I need you to help me.

*

Mice whistle at me in the nighttime, they bite my scalp. But how can I send them away? They smirk at me from restaurant windows. It is hard to maintain the rituals. The boys have their own Gods now. But why must it be so hard to think, to recall?

Especially if I am a cupbearer, as I think I am. What is lacking in me now is clarity of spirit. One must be able to think, if one is to pray. The Gods require attention, when things things things of the world bustle in. I mean crows perched on rotting telegraph poles, I mean an empty chariot, I mean that I can hardly recall the duties I owe to the God of Guides or the God of Form. Hail skitters on glass, though there are no clouds. Do you remember I found this cart a block from a supermarket? It is mine. I wiped myself on your newspaper. Help me to persist.

*

Know what I think, he asked me. I had my hands at my sides. How can I plant where there is no soil? You want to know what I think. Hawklike I watched the hawk. He said: You're a dirty filthy old man, aren't you. You're a dirty filthy horrible old man, that's what I think. I was looking at the bird. You brought me down here to have your wicked way with me, didn't you. Brought me down to your hole because you like to finger little boys, don't you. You like to poke your finger in. I heard steps, I saw figures approaching, but I knew that the God of Tight Corners would protect me. I mumbled the words.

I tried to tell them what a God is. I told them about the wind and the rain. They wanted what they thought to be my drugs. They encircled me, smelling of warfare, twiddling their knives. I thought they might like the God of Travelling Across the Country with Only One Shirt. Their faces perked up and they made jokes about rape and pushed at me. I started to falter. Did the God carry his own spear, or was it his dear friend's? I was lost. Walking through an abandoned house, your foot crashes through the floorboards. They could see it. This is a God, I said to them, with my hands far apart, but it used to be our God. I was thinking of the God of Hermaphroditism. I said: Now it is my God. We have the treatment, my boy said. A God is made by rite and prayer, I said. Do you know what rite and prayer means? The Gods used to come to men at nightfall, I said, by the evening lamp, I said again. We have the treatment for dirty old men, he said. They used to whisper. Threatening murmurs, gobs of snot spitting at my feet. I waited for the God of Steaming or the God of Money to come and tell me.

We have the treatment for dirty filthy old men. We do. Five of them now, faces sweaty, smirking, they were coming closer. We have the treatment. They set about me with brass on their hands. With the first blow I tottered; the pain in my jaw and my neck and shoulder, it made me think of the God Who Withstood Everything. The first kick in my groin clenched me double. Going down I saw the bird, would they use it on me as a weapon, I thought, but they had weapons of their own. Dirty, filthy, they were chanting. I was lying on the floor, they kicked me on to my side and onto my back and onto my front, my organs protested, the vomit filled my bloody mouth. My eye disappeared into its own jelly. I made no effort to protect myself: the God of the Soul Clenched Between Your Teeth.

– Mark F.

MY IDEA OF
PERFECTION

School of Continuing Education:
Introduction to Creative and Reflective Writing

Assignment 1, due class 2
(via email to instructor: damian.tarnopolsky@utoronto.ca)
3–4 pages / max. 1000 words, 12 pt font, double-spaced,
no crazy margins please

A note for the perplexed: Not sure where to start? Read over
the prompt, put your name at the top of the page, then write
for ten minutes without stopping.

What's your idea of perfection? Write about it!

Laura Grolier.

Oh boy. I guess I'd say: I love how silent the house is at six. I bike slowly down through the park, our vizsla, my Jenny, at my side. Perfection. Babies in strollers gaze in wonder at me, their mouths become quasars. Grinding up the driveway I am grateful for the crab apples falling from the tree getting eaten by black squirrels, raccoons, and even bunnies. Then I am grateful for modern plumbing, my hot shower, the smell of coffee, our white bookshelves, our beautiful dog. I never noticed the yellow powder above her loving nose. Now I watch her watch the birds with sleepy eyes. She's always at my feet. I make an omelette and turn it perfectly. It's goopy in the middle, it's crisp at the sides. Is that what you mean, perfection?

I made a secret spreadsheet to track our vacation fund. It tallies up the automatic withdrawal from each client cheque. It puts this number in Column D without prompting and turns it yellow. It tells me how much we've put aside, and what's left unsaved, to be saved. When things go nuts at work I open it. I keep coming back to it. I think maybe I'm a little in love with it. It's taking us to Italy, you see, when all this is over.

They have karate, they have swim. I dash in to the organic grocer quickly during. The receipt with tax comes to $101.01. Sure, I have bags. And there was a spot out front. What are the chances?

And then reading my big new purple novel on our plum-coloured Lombard Street couch, smelly Jenny beside. She needs a bath. I need to get the kids to help me bathe her. I can just hear you banging away with your hammer at the new dog-house roof, and then I can just hear you whistling Elvis. I'm ready for your 'Bryan's in the doghouse' jokes in your grainy voice when it leaks. I fall asleep, I wake up. I'm here, I'm not. You above me, you beneath me. We're different people on the weekend. A cool breeze passes over me.

Out back as the sun sets the warm air supports us. You're sitting here, with me, against me, as I grumble about my dry elbows, we're a wineglass next to a stubby can of amber lager on a wood-deck. Phones black, done for the day, we joke; we're not caught up, but accepting we'll never be caught up. Will you remember to put your tool bag inside, or will it be soaked in dew come morning? I don't ask. I can hear our little daughter's clumpy dance steps on the kitchen tiles through the window, her voice reaches out to us through the hanging branches, she's always just above or just below the line, just like Bella singing in the back seat on our way to camp.

Far away, smoke is rising. It's the day, the day is perfect: it's nothing, it's normal, but it's perfection. You just have to look. You just have to stop.

I feel you getting ready to get up to turn the burgers. The platinum grill tells your wristwatch when it's time; I know your movements better than my own. The poem from class about the mermaids comes into my head: with their hair blown back, when the wind blows the water white and black. I never thought that they would sing to me. I don't say it, because you'd laugh. But it's here, in my head. I love you, but you're not the only man I've ever loved. Oh boy, I need to take that out before sending.

The earth just moved another million miles through frozen space.

I never noticed.

No demons here, no monsters. Not today.

I never noticed.

You laughed when I said I was doing this. You're not the writer in the family, Les said, chewing. But Amy was happy. And everyone at work says I write the best emails. Have you even started? said Les. It's due tomorrow! I've started, I said.

Thank God Milinda left Mark. I mean thank God for her sake. He never figured it out, did he? I mean how to be with other people. How to be with yourself.

My son, my Les, he takes such delight in his scorn. His riposte is always perfectly turned. Yesterday I was changing his diapers on the rug in the living room, landline squeezed tight against my collarbone (I never once held my breath); now he has this wispy moustache. Where are you going? Out. When will you be back? Later. He saunters down the driveway like a linebacker, and he's gone. The world is his.

But like always as my daughter comes out with an orange Bubly she crashes against the door and Jenny startles. I meant that! she insists, as we lock eyes. Amy's just a little clumsy, like Bella was. They look the same. Every time I see it, every time I see Bella's eyes in this face, I want to cry. But today, I just smile.

ACKNOWLEDGMENTS

Earlier versions of the following stories have previously been published as below:

"In the Parlour," *The Antigonish Review* (Spring/Summer 2020)
"You Guys," *Maisonneuve* (Fall 2009)
"In Spain," *Prairie Fire* (Fall 2011)
"Laud We the Gods," *subterrain* (Spring 2009), reprinted in
   The Journey Prize Anthology 22 (2010)
"Like Triumph," *The Ex-Puritan* (Fall 2022)

My thanks to the editors of these journals.

There are sources everywhere, but I should note that in "Hucket's Technic," the setting and the idea of Buddhist philosophy inspiring Hucket's conceptions of the self via Jesuit exploration come originally from Alison Gopnik's article, "Could David Hume Have Known About Buddhism?" Certain other details are drawn from *Sleeping, Dreaming and Dying*, ed. Francisco J. Varela, and various works by Thupthen Jinpa, etc., while other sources on the travels of Ippolito Desideri, Paul Raguneau, Jean de Brebeauf, etc., have their influence, without there being any pretence at historical accuracy. The description of the Native American dream economy is drawn from David Graeber and David Wengrow, *The Dawn of Everything*. In "Handcuffs," Laura's line, "What power may care in comprehending justice for the grief of lovers bound unequally by love?" comes from Robert Fitzgerald's translation of *The Aeneid*.

Several of these stories go back a while and have benefitted from many readers' attention over the years. Most recently, my deep thanks to the Wordsmiths/Short Story Yakkity, especially Nic Billon, Theresa Fuller, Bruce Geddes, Spencer Gordon, Stephen Nickson, Anne Perdue, and Shawn Syms, for their comments on "Like Triumph" and "Hucket's Technic." Enormous thanks to Kelsey Attard, Naomi K. Lewis, Natalie Olsen, Colby Clair Stolson, and all at Freehand for their dedication, brilliance, and kindness. Unending thanks to Jane Warren for her superlative, transformative edit of the first draft, and her warm and unstinting encouragement and guidance since. Final thanks to Gabriel Levine and Leon Lukashevsky for reading these and others and sticking with me, thick and thin; to my parents for, amidst much else, keeping my earliest stories; to Kate, above all and beyond words.

Damian Tarnopolsky is the author of *Lanzmann and Other Stories*, *Goya's Dog*, and *The Defence*. His work has been nominated for many awards, including the Commonwealth Writers' Prize, the Amazon First Novel Award, and the Journey Prize, and he won the Voaden Prize for Playwriting in 2019. He teaches at the Narrative-Based Medicine Lab at the University of Toronto.

ALSO BY DAMIAN TARNOPOLSKY

Lanzmann and Other Stories

Goya's Dog

The Defence